SECOND CHANCES

T. A. WEBB

Dreamspinner Press

Published by
Dreamspinner Press
5032 Capital Circle SW
Ste 2, PMB# 279
Tallahassee, FL 32305-7886
USA
http://www.dreamspinnerpress.com/

Second Chances

Cover Art by Paul Richmond
http://www.paulrichmondstudio.com

ISBN: 978-1-62380-032-1

Printed in the United States of America
First Edition
October 2012

eBook edition available
eBook ISBN: 978-1-62380-033-8

This book is dedicated to four people: Sam Brown, who is family to me and always will be. Talon PS, who loved me and allowed me to love him for the short time we had together—the answer is yes, each and every day. Josh W., who deserved a better life and a happy ending—I hope you found some peace. But mostly to Bernice Webb, my mother, who showed me how to love unconditionally.

ACKNOWLEDGMENTS

I'VE always hated those authors who have a list of people a mile long to thank and think this is the Academy Awards or something. Then I wrote a book that actually was accepted for publication, and that's when it hit me that it's not just *my* book. It's Amy Lane's and Mary Calmes's book, because they were the first to say I could do more than write a nice review and kept at me until I did. It's Carol Zampa's book because she held my hand and told me I didn't suck and kept my focus clear. It's Sue Brown's book because she knew the truth. It's Lee Brazil's and John Goode's book because they read it with their hearts and through the eyes of another man and made it better. It's Laura Harner's book because she was the last set of eyes on it before I hit "Submit" and she held my hand until the acceptance came back. And it belongs most of all to those wonderful young people in foster care I worked with who had scars and bumps and bruises on their souls, but stars in their eyes.

CHAPTER ONE

October 2000

I WONDERED if praying that she wouldn't pull out of this episode made me a terrible son. I didn't dare breathe a word of that to anybody, but fuck it, I could stand here and by God take a minute to suffer and let my heart bleed in private. Pull all the jagged pieces of my soul together and cobble them into something resembling the man everybody knew as Mark Jennings before I had to go in and be him.

But after a few minutes and a few more deep breaths, I pulled it together. Took the piece of me that was the good son, attached it to the responsible work Mark, the peacemaker brother, the single gay man pieces. Looked at all the parts tiredly, and once they fit into something that approached a whole man, I slipped back into my skin. I took a deep breath and opened the door to Mom's room.

Dad was there. It may have been too early for any of my brothers and sisters, but that was almost a relief. Today it would be nice just to have some time with him while I still felt so tired and raw.

"It's good to see you, son." He hugged me and eyed the sack I brought in from Huey's. He loved the beignets and the muffaletta sandwiches I'd gotten into the habit of picking up for our dinner.

I handed him the bag. "You too, Dad. Looks like everything's about the same here, huh? Thought I'd come and keep you company."

"But I know you're tired. I told you to go home after work and I'd call you if anything changed," he fussed as he dug around in the bag.

"Just hush and eat. Where is everybody?" I plopped down in a chair and kicked my shoes off. I'd been at this damn hospital enough to know how to make myself comfortable.

"You're it right now." He plowed into the food like a hungry bear, and I knew he'd probably skipped lunch to sit with her. Again. "Patty was here earlier, and Robert. Said he and Jennifer'd be back tonight. The doctor was in today, said she may wake up tomorrow some time."

I didn't want to talk about that right now. More than anything, that subject threatened the fragile internal balance I'd forged, so we talked about little crap. What my day'd been like. What had to be done around the house when he made it back there.

But we also slid in some of the more important things, too. How was he holding up? Was I okay? Had I heard from Brian? Things he would share with me, the responsible son. My brothers and sisters, while I loved them, always made everything such fucking drama, and found reasons to let me handle the hard things. You know, since I didn't have kids and a wife, or a husband, or a boyfriend. At least that's what Brenda and Sam and Linda thought. Robert and Patty, at least, pitched in as best they could.

But it was also our way to ignore the big things without telling each other to fuck off.

"Go home," he finally sighed. "Get some sleep. I don't want to have to visit you in the hospital, too. You aren't doing her any good wearing yourself out like this." He turned that look on me that still made me want to give up my secrets like I did when I was a kid.

"Backatcha old man," I shot back. "You know she's gonna peel the hide off you for not taking care of yourself. And then it's me that's gonna catch hell for letting you stay here too long. Go home and take a shower, feed that damn cat of hers."

"Shut the fuck up and don't let the door hit ya where the good Lord split ya." He smiled. *I love you, son.*

"Hush up, you dirty old man." I grinned back at him, using Mom's favorite admonition. *I love you, too, Daddy.*

Good Southern boys always made everyone at ease and happy. Who were we to fight what was in our blood? We were pleasant, manly, and only said the hard things and showed our emotions, man to man, when we abso-fucking-lutely had to. But finally, I hugged my old man and took him by surprise when I kissed his cheek and left.

I SAT in the parking deck, alone. Nobody else was around on the whole level. My mind wandered. It touched on seeing Mom in that damned bed, still in a coma. Then to work, and all I needed to get done and hadn't. And then to my family, bless their hearts.

But all I could think about was that damn volleyball.

It was still and quiet, and if I thought about it hard enough, I was Tom Hanks from that damn *Castaway* movie, all alone on the island with nothing but the volleyball he named Wilson to keep me company. All that was missing was the water. Well, and the whole nobody around for miles thing, but that would be a relief.

I could picture a beach, and how nice it'd be to not have any of the responsibilities, any of the heartaches. I'd miss some things, of course. Indoor plumbing. Wings. Takeout Chinese. And that made me think about my dogs, Ricky and Lucy, and how they'd be begging for pieces of the mu shu. That, of course, led to how much they loved to go visit my parents' house and run around in the yard. Then the whole tropical getaway thing just kind of faded away and left me… right back where I started.

But I'd rather be anywhere than *here*. *Here* meant I had to deal with what was in the hospital. *Here* meant spend one more fucking day watching my mom die a little piece at a time. *Here* was being the rock that I always was. *Here* I fixed things.

What I really felt like doing was screaming, "Can't you see I'm going under?" Every step of every day felt like dragging my feet through mud. Like ghosting through the day in slow motion, where either people saw me and gave me those fucking looks of pity, or didn't see me bleeding all over the floor.

It felt like being buried in concrete that was slowly drying around me, hardening 'til I wouldn't have to move ever again. And I didn't know what was worse. To show up at the AIDS service organization where I worked and pull all my wits together. Stay sharp so I didn't make a major fuckup and some client lost his benefits. Try to ignore all the sympathetic looks and words I couldn't afford to let in. Or open myself up and drown in them.

Was it worse to show up and try to be the dutiful son and brother and nephew? Do all the right things, say all the right words to ease everybody else's pain. Let everyone drain me a bit more every minute of every day of what little resources I had left. Take and take and take from me and never give back.

No, to be alone during all this was the worst. Nobody there to be my rock. Nobody to hear it when I needed to talk or shout. Nobody to tell me it would be okay and hold me for just a minute so I didn't have to go in the shower and let the hot water burn the day out of my skin so I could pretend my skin felt alive and touched again. I might've kicked Brian out, but fuck, wouldn't it've been better to have half a relationship than the empty house waiting for me every night?

So was it any fucking wonder I sat in the car, gripped the steering wheel, and thought about being Tom fucking Hanks? That I wanted to be anybody but that man who had to see my mother suffer one more day? Yeah, dying of liver disease was a slow, cold-assed way to go. But it was just as hard on those who were waiting and being sucked dry.

But after a few minutes and a few more deep breaths, I pulled it together and said a wistful good-bye to Wilson. I lifted my head from where it had been leaning on the steering wheel, cranked the car, and made my way out of the parking deck and home.

THE first thing I did when got to the house was put the dogs out, then kicked my shoes off. I hated wearing shoes and was known to be barefooted in the dead of winter. Mom loved to tell the story of when she bought me my first pair of shoes as a toddler. I kicked my feet and tried to shake them off and cried. Some things never change, I guess.

At least now I remembered to keep my underwear on when I ran outside for the mail.

I grabbed a beer and put fresh food and water down for the babies. The house was so quiet once the pups settled down, and I wasn't in the mood for television. I sat there in the silence and rolled my neck to try to loosen the tightness so I could think. About tomorrow, about what would happen when Mom woke up. About Brian, for the millionth time. Shit, I needed something to make my brain stop the fucking spinning.

The sun set, and my one beer turned into three. I felt a little looser, not so itchy in my skin again. Stopped looking up for someone to walk in and break the silence. Lucy and Ricky curled up on the couch asleep. I was too awake to go to bed, but too buzzed to get dressed and go back out.

Maybe a hot shower would relax me. I stripped down, got the water as hot as I could take it, and stepped into the stall. I'd bought one of those CD players that you can hang from the towel bar and listen to music on. It felt like a Jackson Browne type of night, so "The Pretender" carried through the sound of the water as it rained down on me. I reached out of the shower stall to flick the light switch off and just breathed in some peace there in the dark of the evening.

The hot water did its magic, and the muscles in my neck relaxed, then my shoulders and chest and back. The noise in my head calmed down and I started to just concentrate on my body, reaching for something besides the grief that lived in me almost bone-deep. I rubbed the washcloth up and down my arms and chest, soaping up my nipples. The heat kept them from tightening up too much, but the friction started the blood moving south, too. Rubbing a little harder got my cock's attention, and he decided to join the party.

I moved the action down and soaped my crotch up nice and slick. Usually I preferred to jack off dry, always have. The friction was so nice and warm and quick. More and more lately I found myself getting hard in the shower, probably because Brian liked it that way. Anytime I climbed in and he was home, it would only take a few minutes 'til the curtain pulled back and his grinning ass came in, never asking, just grabbing the soap and dropping it.

"Oops," he would say, "guess I'd better get that." And he would, either angling against me so his hot ass was right up against my crotch, or falling to his knees right in front of my cock. And of course, I could never resist that temptation.

"Relax, baby, let me take care of you," he'd say. I'd lean back against the cool tiles as he ran his fingers through the hair on my chest, down my abs to my pubes. His soft touch intermingled with scratches, lazy figure eights in the fur on my front that made me lean back and close my eyes and enjoy the sensation.

"Mmm, God, I love the hair here," he'd whisper, almost lost in the noise of the water. I'd spread my legs a little wider, and his hot mouth would ghost across my balls, breathing warm air on them, not touching yet, while those light touches on my abdomen would slowly change to both hands rubbing up and down my thighs. My cock would slowly rise, and I'd feel his mouth lightly touching my balls, the barest flicker of tongue on them. This slow seduction was always my favorite.

I reached down and gave my cock a quick squeeze and grabbed my balls with the other hand. Light tugging did the job, and I got fully hard. One hand stroked up and down my shaft lazily, and I could almost feel his mouth on me even now.

"Suck it," I'd say. He'd chuckle, and one ball would get sucked into the hot cavern of his mouth and I'd sigh. I knew he could never resist when I started telling him what to do. The game was always to see how long I could take it before I gave the order. His mouth sucking one ball, then the other, he'd rub his nose against my shaft, smelling the musk there. I could always look down and see his cock harden as he sniffed and nuzzled mine, moving his attention from my balls up to its root. Mouthing the base, then moving slowly up my shaft, then back down he would lick and nibble and mouth every bit of skin he could reach.

"I said suck it, boy." His cock would jerk, and he'd look up at me and beg with his eyes. "No, you can't touch yourself 'til you take care

of this first." I'd say, twisting my hips back and forth, slapping my cock against his face.

The memory made my cock harden 'til it was almost painful. I'm not sure what turned me on most, the look in his eyes or the feel of his mouth opening and taking in the head and a couple of inches. I started stroking harder, remembering how beautiful his mouth looked, those lips wrapped around my cock, his eyes begging for my approval. My hand moved faster.

I'd shove him backward against the tile wall until his head was trapped, my cock moving in and out of his mouth.

I stroked harder and faster, feeling the tension in my balls and spine start to build. My hips started that unconscious pumping that always added to the friction, and the tightness of my grip and the slickness of the water almost, *almost* felt like a mouth. Almost but not quite, and I fucked my hand harder.

I shoved more and more into Brian's mouth until the need became too hot and heavy and the flame of my orgasm burned in my spine and then I came in his mouth.

With a gasp, I shot onto the shower curtain, the release making my knees weak, until the last shuddering spasm passed and I could breathe again and open my eyes.

And remembered his lying, cheating ass was gone and I was alone.

WORK the next day was no better. I was controller for a small nonprofit, and it was right at the busy time of year for our two largest fund-raising drives. So of course the development folks couldn't get anything done without me approving protocols and making reports and generally holding their crazy little hands. God save me from Type B personalities. My weekend would be taken up running back and forth between the hospital and supervising the setup for the AIDS Fun-Run and then home to take the dogs out and feed them.

Something had to give. I sat in my boss's office and glared a hole through Dan Martin. Not that the bastard cared. He was one of the nicest, most fair men I knew, but work was work.

"How's your mother, Mark?" he asked. He looked at me as though staring hard enough would make all my secrets tumble out.

"Fine." I knew I was being an ass but couldn't seem to help it.

"Oookay, let's try this again. How's your mother? Asshole," he drawled.

Even I wasn't able to keep up the stink eye against his starched shirt and perfect Windsor knot and calm demeanor. Fucker.

"She's holding her own. The doctor says that we have some really hard choices to make when she wakes up. Her body can't take much more of the back and forth. It's really just a matter of time." My throat tightened up and the words came out flat. I knew my eyes were wet, but damn it, I wouldn't cry. Not today. Not here.

"I *am* sorry," he said quietly. He was no more a fan of public displays of emotions than me. "And I'm sorry you're having to carry some of the load on the fun-run and the ball fund-raisers. I promise I'll make it up to you. There just isn't anybody else right now. Since you let Jim go, I know you're doing two people's jobs and believe me, Mark, I won't forget it."

He looked me up and down. "Take care of yourself. Have you thought about a massage? I can give you the number of the girl I use."

Yeah, like I wanted some girl's hands on me like that. Nothing personal, but I'd yet to find a woman who knew how to deliver a good massage. Their hands just weren't strong enough for me. I liked the deep tissue stuff, and that took a man.

"Not yet. I appreciate it, but between the seven days a week I'm putting in here, and the trips back and forth to Piedmont, I'm lucky to spend any time with the dogs and get my laundry done." I laughed. "I wish I could train them to start the washer and push the vacuum. Or make dinner."

"Think about it. I can tell you need to do something for yourself. And don't argue with me. I know what you're going through." And he did. He'd lost his mother two years before. "Now go home. It's lunchtime, and I think I can cover for you today. Do something for yourself before you have to go back to the hospital. And I'll see you tomorrow. Go." He flipped his hand and motioned me out.

For once, he didn't have to tell me twice. I got.

I FIRED up the computer at home and hit the web. Dan's words made an impact. Maybe a massage *would* be the best thing I could do for myself. Since *Creative Loafing*, the weekly lifestyle magazine, was now all ads for hookers, maybe some massage guys hung out in the "Atlanta MM4MM" room. The M4M room would be full of guys looking for hookups and prostitutes. I'd had enough of that.

And damn if I wasn't right. There were five different massage guys in there. I put a query out in the chat room.

MarkBearAtl: *Who does deep tissue? Real massage, not just squirt lotion on and go for the happy ending. 'Cause you will NOT get paid.*

I went to put in a load of laundry, and when I get back, there were three chat windows open.

MassageManAtl: *$100 per hour, nude massage happy ending.*

Ah, no. Hit the X.

AtlRubsU: *How big are you hung?*

Nope. X.

ItalMassageAtl: *Hello MarkBearAtl, how are you today? Having a good day?*

Huh.

MarkBearAtl: *Yes. How are you today?*

ItalMassageAtl: *Having a really nice day, thanks. Are you looking for a serious massage?*

MarkBearAtl: *Yes. Have a lot of stress. Need some relief. Deep tissue, hot stone, whatever will work on my neck and back.*

ItalMassageAtl: *Well, man, I offer deep tissue, professional massage table, shower available. And by massage, I MEAN massage. No happy ending stuff. Do you have any health issues I should be aware of?*

MarkBearAtl: *No, just really tense. What are your rates?*

ItalMassageAtl: *$100 for a full hour. I don't do less than an hour, because you deserve the best and I am the best.*

Well, no lack of confidence there.

MarkBearAtl: *Can you see me this evening? Around 8?*

ItalMassageAtl: *I have an opening. I do require that we talk on the phone first. I have to feel comfortable knowing you are really going to show up. And you aren't an ax murderer.*

MarkBearAtl: *Damn, found me out. LOL Okay, what's your number?*

And that was how I met Antonio.

CHAPTER TWO

THE drive to the hospital was long and traffic sucked. I dreaded what might be waiting for me there, and as I got closer, I steeled myself for the news. As I parked the car, I saw that my dad and older sister were already there, judging from the cars. Usually, we all parked on the same level in the deck. Walking into Mom's room, I was thankful that it was just the two of them. They were obviously waiting for me to get there.

And Mom was awake.

"Hey, son," she said, voice raw and loud. She'd been in a coma for three days, so no surprise there. The volume—well, more hearing loss, I could tell. Her hair was matted down, her color looked like hell, and her skin was sagging and dry. I don't think I had ever seen anyone so beautiful.

"How are you feeling, darlin'?" I grabbed her in a big hug.

"Sore. Tired. I want to go home. They're going to let me go home." She smiled that smile that made everything all right.

No fucking way was she going to be able to come home. I looked back at Dad and Patricia and raised an eyebrow. Dad looked at me, saying nothing.

Patty's eyes glided past me and she took a deep breath. "Come outside with me for minute, little brother." She and my dad followed me out, glancing at each other and then at me.

"So, she's coming home? Talk to me." I looked at Dad.

"I promised her she could die at home. I won't let her die in a hospital. Not gonna happen." His jaw was set, his eyes fierce.

"The doctor said he didn't think she would make it out of one more episode, and it was her choice," Patty's sweet voice told me. "She wants to go home."

Fuck. You know that feeling when you hold your breath too long and the little squigglies start to dance right around the outside of your vision and voices start to sound a little hollow? Well, that shit started and a part of me just… went away for a minute, and I thought, *Okay Mark, you can do this. Just let her have what she wants and say it's okay and then we can get the holy hell out of here.*

I took a deep breath to steady myself and looked at them. "So how's this gonna work? We take her home and she does what, goes into a coma? How do we take care of her? Did the doctor say we could?"

Dad's relieved look slowed me down. The two of them relaxed, and I figured they'd expected me to fight them on this. Fuck no. I wanted Mom happy. If she wanted to die at home, then God help the asshole who tried to stop it from happening. We discussed details for another minute, and then went back in to talk to Mom.

She was so happy, and kept saying over and over, "They're letting me go home. I'm going home."

I looked over at Patty and asked the hardest question. "Do the rest of them know?"

Our little brother Robert was fighting the doctors tooth and nail about her care. Janet and Linda were playing the passive-aggressive bitch card, either wanting to make the rest of us miserable by objecting and finding fault with everything we did or totally ignoring the situation. And Sam, well, he tried to tell us all how it was going to be— the gospel according to Saint Sam. Screw 'em.

And no, they didn't know yet.

"I have my cell phone." I shrugged. "Let's start making the calls."

"I'm going *home*!"

I LEFT about half after seven. My head and back and heart ached. For a minute, as I pulled out of the parking deck, I considered blowing off the massage and going and getting shitfaced. But I had to work the next day, and no damn way was I gonna get a DUI. What if Mom came home and went back into a coma and then died and I was in jail because I was being stupid and… nope. Not gonna go there.

So I kept driving, pulled out my cell to call Antonio, and let him know I was on my way. I could feel the tension in my neck and arms and thought, *I really need this*.

I pulled into the parking lot at the apartment complex at five minutes 'til eight. Got out and went right up to the door and knocked. I stood there for a minute and let the cool Atlanta night air fill my lungs. Looked around the courtyard and admired the fountain and the landscaping.

I didn't remember this place being here last time I was in the Cheshire Bridge area. There used to be titty bars and head shops and a couple of bathhouses there back in the day. But not now—the streets were cleaner and the units were nice, graffiti-free and brand-new. The door opened and *hot damn*, that was Antonio?

He was almost six feet tall, head shaved with just a light peach fuzz starting to grow back in. Sharp Roman nose and angular features, tattoos on his forearms and neck. Deep-set blue eyes. I couldn't really tell much about the body because he was wearing a T-shirt about three sizes too big and sleep pants and no shoes. And a huge smile.

"Mark, glad to meet you, man." His voice was nice, deep, no trace of an accent. "Come in."

I walked in and looked around. There wasn't much furniture in the place, a leather couch and loveseat, a table in the dining area, a six foot table with a laptop and printer and God knows what all attached to it that took up the whole space. The kitchen area, right off the entryway, looked empty. All I saw there was a microwave and coffeemaker. Nothing else on the counters.

Off to one side, there was a hallway with what looked like two bedrooms, both doors closed, and a bath. There was a little sunroom with great windows on three sides, covered with mini blinds. In it sat a massage table. The lighting was low and there was Enya on the stereo. Of course.

"Sit down and let's talk for a few minutes. Want something to drink?" he asked.

"Sure. Have some water?"

He pointed to the sofa and motioned for me to sit, and went into the kitchen. Damn, still couldn't tell much about his ass with those baggy sleep pants. Oh well, I was here for a massage anyway, I thought.

He came back with a bottle of water for me and a glass of red wine for himself. Italian men and wine—what a damned nice combination. Made my mind wander and I thought about villas and vineyards and pasta. Wonder if he cooks too?

"So talk to me, Mark. What do you do? What brings you here?" He sat on the other end of the sofa.

"I handle all the financial stuff for a nonprofit, and right now it's driving me crazy. Too much to do and not enough manpower to make it happen. I'm working almost every day, and have been for the past two months. Some personal shit's going on too, so my stress level's off the charts right now." I took a swallow of water.

He glanced at me, looking up and down my body, and damn if that didn't make me flush a little. "Well, we can definitely do something about that tonight. Sounds like you work way too hard. Can't someone else help? Hope you're getting paid for it at least."

I laughed hard. "Riiight. I work for a nonprofit. That means I take what little they offer and work 'til I drop. But yeah, I can handle it, because it doesn't happen like this all the time. It's just a really stressful time right now."

He reached over and squeezed my forearm and looked me right in the eye. "Yeah, I understand all that, but who's making sure you take care of yourself? Because you can't do it all alone."

Damn. The focus in his eyes was almost unnerving. I was only here for the massage, but this guy seemed to want to know more than I wanted to share.

But really, how long was it since somebody sat down and actually asked about *me*? God, I felt so pathetic sometimes. Since I kicked Brian out in January, it'd been months since I'd spent time anywhere other than at work, with Mom or the family, or at home. And the dogs, they don't talk so much.

"It'll be okay. I have another two weeks of serious long days, and then it'll ease up. But then I have to think about—" and I stopped. He didn't need to know about Mom.

But he caught it and asked, "What?"

"Nothing. Just… other things. So tell me about you. You make good money doing this? Has to be hard, there must be a thousand massage guys in this city." I laughed. "I know I talked to two others earlier when we were chatting and I see the chat rooms full every damn time I'm online."

He frowned. "It's hard as hell. Most of those guys on there call themselves massage therapists, but not a damn one of them are licensed. I am." He pointed to a framed certificate on the wall over his computer. "They also fucking undercut me and charge fifty bucks for a session, and from what I hear all you get's a quick rubdown and a handjob, and sent on your way after twenty minutes. With me, you get a great massage for an hour and there isn't any funny business."

I didn't know whether to say *Amen* or *Shit*. "You must be doing okay, though. This's a nice property here, and the rent can't be cheap."

"I do okay." He shrugged. "Business is steady, and I get a lot of callbacks. I prefer to do incalls so I don't have to lug the table around, but outcalls can make me a lot more money. It covers the rent, bills and child support."

So that answers *that* question. Straight. Maybe bi but telling me *that* this early was shutting it down. Straight. Well, good. It's not like I had a chance with a guy like this, anyway.

I mean, I'm okay, but nothing to write home about. A couple of inches over six feet tall, furry. Not built, and in fact a couple of extra pounds from eating way too much takeout lately and not enough exercise. Buzz cut and a goatee. But I'm told my best feature is my steely gray eyes that have the tint of blue in them.

"You have a…?" I left it open-ended.

"Son. He's eight years old. Lives with his mom and her boyfriend in Alpharetta. And no, I am not gay. Or bi." His eyes laughed at me. Fucker. "Love the ladies. Especially after they've been walking in their high heels around the mall for a few hours shopping. You know what I mean."

His grin was contagious.

"No, really can't say as I do. Maybe a guy who's been working out at the gym for a couple of hours and's in the sauna, though," I volleyed. Ball in your court now, young son.

"You say potato, I say po-*tah*-to," he laughed. "You told me you don't have any health issues to worry about. Any specific areas you want me to focus on?"

"My neck and lower back are killing me, to be honest. With all this worrying about my mom, I haven't had a good night's sleep in two months." Damn it, I was getting too comfortable here. With him. What the fuck was wrong with me?

"Something's wrong with your mom?" His concern sounded real.

Damn. I thought about it for a long minute, and took a deep breath. Fuck it.

"She's dying. She has liver failure and she was in a coma and she just woke up today and we're taking her home and she's going to die in the next little while." It all came out in one rushed mouthful, all flat and solid. I hoped.

His look was unexpected. Compassion, without pity. Caring, sympathetic even. Those blue eyes saw me, and it felt good to be… connected.

"I lost my dad when I was a teenager. I remember how tough it is." He stood up and reached down for my hand. "Come on, let me take care of you."

Lying bare-assed on a massage table wasn't something I was used to. I liked, *needed*, to be in control, and this was an uncomfortable position. Antonio moved around behind me, then away. There was a ding from the microwave and he was back. I heard a pop from a lid, a wet noise, and I thought, *Oh God*. This was too close to something I hadn't had in too long.

Then there was warm oil on my back, and big strong hands moved across my shoulders and the back of my neck. I felt the muscles there unknot and relax, and by the time he moved to my arms there was a little bit of drool falling from my mouth.

His hands could have bent metal. Ripped car doors off. Punched holes in brick walls. They were warm and healing and oh-so-strong. And then he had me turn over. My whole body felt like spaghetti noodles boiled for an hour. I lost track of time as the worry faded.

His hands started again on my chest and arms, and what little tension I carried in me melted away. I finally opened my eyes a little and he'd taken his shirt off. God, he was beautiful. A light dusting of hair across a solid chest and stomach, not ripped but looking like a man who worked with his body for a living. Total concentration on his face. If I wasn't so relaxed I'd have popped a boner. My eyes closed again and I drifted along with… The Carpenters?

He liked The Carpenters? *Well, I'll be damned.* Those hands made me forget about that, too. He worked on my fingers, squeezed and rubbed. He moved up my arms, then down to my thighs. My calves unknotted under his touch and then my feet. Damn, he spent about ten minutes just on my feet. I thought I'd fall asleep. It felt like I was floating.

Just when I thought he was finished, there was a warm, slick hand on my crotch. I started, moved to get up, but then I heard his voice. "Shhh. Let me take care of you. It's okay. It's been a tough day. Shhh." And I relaxed and let it happen.

I didn't even open my eyes. Just laid there and felt his strong hands rub my balls and run up and down my dick. As it hardened, he added a little more warm oil and stroked.

In slow, long strokes, his warm, sure hand ran from the root of my cock to the head. The pressure was just right, and before I knew it the orgasm eased out of me gently, no more than a sigh compared to others that made me scream out and cuss. But it was just what I needed.

"Stay." He pressed one hand on my chest like he was holding me to the table somehow, and his steps faded as he moved away. Water ran, and he was back with a washcloth, gently cleaning me off.

"Lay there for a couple of minutes, then get up and you can get dressed. I'm going to get you another bottle of water and me some wine and we can talk."

I SAT on the couch, relaxed but a little unsettled. What the fuck just happened? My gaydar was either broken or he flew the hell under it. Or he was straight but… something? I glanced down at my watch and saw I'd been there over two hours. He came back in, closed the door, and sat down on the loveseat.

"Feeling better? How's your stress level? The back better?" he asked.

"Yeah. Gonna sleep like a baby tonight." I looked up and didn't see anything on his face but concern. Maybe a little curiosity and a little excitement.

"I've got something I want to show you. If you have a minute. It's something that means a lot to me and I think you might like it."

How could I say no? I nodded.

"Okay," he said, and went to the computer table and came back with what looked like a deck of cards. He took them out of the box and started shuffling them.

"These're angel cards. There's a meaning that's specific to each card. Here," he fanned the deck out. "Pick three. They'll tell you what you need in your life right now."

I pulled out three at random and looked. Compassion. Hope. Healing.

He looked up the meanings in a small book and read them to me. I only heard his voice, not the words, because the cards themselves were works of art. Each had a beautiful painting. A beautiful angel with wings, comforting a man in distress. Laying on hands. Hugging.

It was all too much. And too close to home. I stood up and knew I needed to get going.

"Antonio, thank you so much for the massage," I blurted. "It was just what I needed, and I feel like a million bucks. But I'm about to fall asleep, and I have to work in the morning."

I counted out a hundred and fifty bucks and gave to him. To my surprise, he tossed the money on the counter, not counting it and grabbed me in a rough hug.

"I like you, Mark, and I hope you'll come see me again. You're a nice guy and you have an old soul. I hope we can be friends."

What. The. Fuck?

"I'd like that." I was confused, and shit, *way* too tired and drained to think.

"Call me to let me know you got home. I don't like that you have to drive." He looked concerned as he walked me to the door.

I just stared, nodded, and left before something truly fucked up came out of my mouth.

But I called him when I got home to let him know I was safe.

CHAPTER THREE

December 2000

I'D BEEN back to see Antonio several times since that massage. It was funny though, neither of us ever acknowledged that he jerked me off. It hadn't happened again, and I didn't know whether to be relieved or pissed off.

I scheduled for eight in the evening every time, and he seemed to be okay with it. It let me take care of the things I needed to do—finish work, feed my dogs, then drive back into the city. But I never spent less than three hours there.

We always took a while to talk before he started the massage. "How was your day? How's your mom?" were always the first questions he asked. The fact that someone, anyone, was concerned about me was nice. And I felt really comfortable around him, more than I thought I would as a client. I think that's why I started taking the glass of wine he offered. But no damn way was I going to let him put ice cubes in *my* merlot. That shit was wrong. And nasty.

So I took the wine and filled him in on the news. Bitched about work, told him how the week had gone. Because, yeah, Dan had been right and the massages *did* help me manage my stress. The conversation made me feel human again.

The news was always worse, so I needed to know someone besides my family cared, even if it was someone I didn't really know. Maybe that's what made it easier. Work, at least, had eased off some. The two big events were over, and there was only one more fancy, schmancy fund-raiser on New Year's Eve left, but I knew that Mom's battle would be over before then.

So we'd spend about an hour talking, shooting the shit about my day, my life, growing up in Atlanta. Anything. And I learned about him. How he was originally from Los Angeles. Stayed out of the gang stuff, joined the Army after high school. Was a Ranger but hated authority, so only stayed in for one tour.

Moved around the country. His favorite place was Arizona. He hinted he did illegal things—gunrunning, low-level organized crime shit. Made tons of money then turned around and blew it as soon as it got in his hands. "I was a wild man, fucking out of control," he said. Partied wild and crazy in Vegas, fucked every girl he could find, sometimes two or three at a time. Lots of drinking and drugs and who knows what else.

"So what got you in the massage business, then? You can't be making the bucks you made then doing this. Especially if you take three hours with every client," I finally asked him one night. It was late, after he gave me another killer massage—strictly massage—that drained every last bit of tension from my tired and sore body.

He looked at me a little funny. "I don't take three hours with all my clients. Just you. You aren't just a client. You're a friend."

I didn't know what to say to that, so I just kept quiet. He waited a minute before going on with his story.

"It was all good, then I met this one chick when I was here in Atlanta making a delivery. Jeanine was hot, and I needed to get laid. I fucked her and forgot the damn rubber. Fucking tequila." He stopped and drank some wine.

"She got pregnant and then I had a kid on the way. Sooner or later the shit I was doing would've caught up with me, and no kid of mine is gonna go without a dad." He sounded fierce, his eyes burning.

His hands clenched and unclenched as he remembered. "So I said fuck it, and moved here. Married her. Bought a house. I had a lot of the last payoff left and that got us settled. It worked for a little while, but when Jason was born, it all went to hell."

He stopped and took a long drink of his wine. "Want some more?"

"No, I have to drive home soon and work tomorrow. I'm so damn mellowed out it'd make me fall asleep right here," I said.

"No problem," he told me. "You want to take a nap, I'll wake you up."

I sure as hell didn't need that. I didn't know why, and was too tired to think about it, but it really wasn't a good idea. "No, that's cool, I'll be fine. Just give me a bottle of water and finish your story."

He settled back down after pouring himself another glass of red wine on the rocks. I shuddered.

"Her dad is some big shot doctor and he kept talking to her and telling her what a piece of shit I was. She finally listened to him, I guess. Let's face it; I'm not the easiest guy to get along with. I couldn't find a job. Who the hell's going to hire a guy with no college, gangstered up with all the tattoos and no fucking résumé? So we split up, and she took Jason with her."

He sat there for a few minutes lost in his memories. His face was blank, but I could see his jaw worked with emotion just under the surface. Those blue eyes were stormy.

"She wanted to keep him away from me. She was fucking this guy, and I came in on it when I went to pick Jason up. I beat the shit out of the guy for doing it in front of my boy. She had me arrested, filed a restraining order, and social services kept me from my baby." His voice was gravel. I didn't dare say anything.

"I had to hire a private detective to prove she was screwing around while Jason was in the house. After I had proof, I hired a lawyer and fought her. It took me two years and three months, but I sat in the courtroom and faced her and her fucking father and all their shit down and I won. I get to see my son every week and two weeks in the summer and two weeks in the winter."

This was the most I'd ever heard him say at one time. I hung on every word though, wanting to know more about this guy. I told myself it was because he was so kind and concerned about me and my mom. But he fucking fascinated me.

"I was broke, but I'd gotten my massage license after I got out of the army. This girl I was with at the time liked it when I massaged her. It took me a while but I'm building a pretty good client base. Lots of repeat business. I use some of the gay hook up sites for travelers and advertise there. I do outcalls to the hotels and charge those guys double, do a massage, and then get my ass out of there." He threw his head back and laughed.

I gave him a long look. "But you aren't gay. Or bi."

"Nope, but these guys don't know that. And all I ever promise is a massage. Cash up front. I get my money, they get their massage, and I get out. I'm a good-looking dude. If they wanna jack off afterwards…." He shrugged. Jacking off. No elephant in the room about *that*.

That made me think for a moment. He didn't exactly lie, but he didn't tell the truth, either. And from what he told me of his past escapades, if I believed ten percent of it, he liked playing fast and loose with the rules.

I needed to keep that in mind. I knew about men who skirted around the truth and looked me in the eyes and lied by omission. Fucking Brian Jacobs. That burned the light buzz I had from the massage and the wine right out of my blood. I needed to remember that as much as I liked this guy, I was still a client.

"Right. Well, it's late and I guess I better get home. I need to check my messages and make sure everything's okay." I pulled my cell phone out and turned it back on and saw I had fifteen missed calls.

My stomach dropped and my head swam. I slowly dialed into voicemail and waited to hear the news I'd been trying to escape tonight.

"IT'S okay, you can let go now," I crooned softly over and over as I stroked her hair.

Mom was in a hospice, because no matter how much we loved her, there was no way our family could deal with the ugly fucking reality of her dying at home. How could my dad ever sleep in their bed again knowing she died in it? And from what the home health nurse said, it could be bloody if… well, we made the decision for hospice and let her go where someone could help us.

It was about five in the morning, the day after my parents' wedding anniversary. It had snowed. She always loved the snow. In Atlanta, we don't get it very often, and it was a big deal. She'd scoop it up in a bowl, add vanilla and a little milk and sugar, and make snow ice cream. I adored her and now my heart was in ashes.

She held on through the night, as if to keep Dad from having to deal with her dying on their anniversary. After sitting and holding her hand for the past four days, would it really have mattered in the long run? Maybe, in the years to come, we'd remember it differently, but now? Fuck it. It's funny where the mind wanders when you're waiting for death to take someone you love.

The best thing about knowing what was coming? I got to sit and talk and let her know every damn thing about me and say what I needed to say and hear what I needed to hear. And so did she, and we cried and hugged and she said she loved me. She knew I needed to hear that. She'd told me that every day of my life, in one way or another.

On my birthday, every year since I turned eighteen, she called me at twelve twenty in the morning to wish me happy birthday and tell me how much joy I brought her. She'd told me she was sorry she couldn't do it when I turned thirty, and handed me a box filled with little bits of paper. She'd written *Happy Birthday to my baby boy* on every one. There must have been fifty of them.

We sat in the darkened room, just a few of us touching her where we could. Christmas lights I'd draped around the head of her bed swirled red and yellow and green slowly around the room. No Christmas tree. She wasn't going to make it to Christmas, and no way did we want to associate Christmas with her death. We took turns talking to her, telling her she could go.

I knew *she* was gone; she'd been for a couple of days. Her body just didn't know it, but I figured she was still connected to it somehow. She just needed to let go and leave. It really was okay, and I was ready for it.

I stroked her hair, sitting there next to the head of the bed. Leaning in, I kept my voice soothing. "It's okay, Momma. Let go. Just let go."

She drew one more breath, let it out, and didn't take another one.

I DIDN'T go back to see Antonio for another month.

The funeral was fucking horrible, of course. How do you sit there and watch the shell of someone who gave you life get put in the ground?

And the cherry on the shit sundae of the clusterfuck that this nightmare had become? Linda's pastor was going to do the service. And he evidently didn't like *The Gay*. Linda, my sister, the one who shared blood with me and sat next to me holding my hand while we cried and said prayer after prayer that Mom would go quickly, that family betrayed me.

Yes, I said prayers. When you stand at the abyss, you fall to your knees and you fucking grab for any comfort, any little thing to keep it from swallowing you whole. You grab it with both hands and you wrestle the bitch to the ground and you force mercy from it.

But my flesh and blood pulled me aside and asked me not to let the pastor know I was, you know, like *that*. Like I was gonna wear a rainbow suit? Blow a strange man on the altar while the eulogy went on? Offer to fuck the pastor?

"Fine," I finally agreed, so disgusted I couldn't look at her. "He says one word out of line, though, and you don't even want to know what I'll do. Our mother, the same one lying in there waiting to be buried, loved me for who I am. If you and this pissant fuckwad can't, that's *your* problem, not mine. I'm here to bury my mother."

Then, oh yes, then Brian came in. The fucker had to look good, didn't he? Dark blue suit, almost black, like his hair, tight across that chest of his. Those pants, not really hiding that nice, tight, round ass. Somber, red-rimmed blue eyes.

And that's what snapped me out of whatever the hell I was thinking, paying attention to how he looked. How dare he cry? How fucking dare he?

He made his way over to me, walking very slowly as if he knew what was going through my head. Hell, he probably did. He'd known me for almost ten years after all. Not all of that was as my lover. We'd been friends at one time, but not now.

"What the fuck are you doing here?" I growled at him. Yes, *growled*. "I didn't call you. I thought you and what's-his-name were in New York."

My body trembled with rage. I gripped the back of a pew to keep my hands from reaching for him.

"Mark, I came as soon as your dad called me," he murmured so quietly, his face so sad.

My head imploded, so bury me too. There might just be two funerals today. Or three, if I killed either Dad or Brian. Maybe both, I thought a little hysterically. We can have four funerals and they can just stack us all in that one plot and it'll all be over with. And I won't have to see this, this *fucker* again.

"I don't want you here. I'm burying my mother," I rasped out, the words sticking like burrs in my mouth.

"I loved her and she loved me," he said with dignity. "She called me the last time she left the hospital and told me she forgave me." And with that his composure cracked. He looked... lost, and I saw the hurt. In spite of my own grief, I ached for him.

His father hadn't wanted him when he found out his son was a fag, and left. Then his mother went off looking for his father one evening and left Brian to fend for himself. After three days, the neighbors saw Brian was there alone and called the police. He was twelve, and the authorities put him into foster care 'til he turned eighteen.

And my mother, with her huge and loving heart that we were there to celebrate on that cold and windy fuck of a day, welcomed him into her home from the moment I brought him by. This was when we were still just friends, introduced by a couple we knew. We kept running into each other at parties and dinner and even shopping.

She invited him in, feeding his body with breakfasts and suppers, and his soul with family. She sent him home with leftovers and pie, and made sure he knew he was loved. Because there was always enough love in her house for another one of my strays.

I forgot. Jesus fucking Christ, he loved her. And I couldn't deny him the chance to let say good-bye. Even I wasn't that much of a cold-hearted bastard. If she could forgive him, and Dad could call him in the middle of all his grief, then I could unclench my heart for an hour and let him grieve too.

"Fine. She'd want you to sit with the family. Come on." I grabbed him by the hand and turned around to take him to the front pew to sit with the family. With me. And ran right into my loving little bitch of a sister.

"Linda." I let my voice get cold, like a glacier sliding up the aisle.

"Mark, I thought we talked about—" she started, her face pinched.

"Get the fuck out of my way," I stopped her, each word an icicle. Brian looked back and forth between us and started to move backward. I still had him by the hand and pulled him right up beside me.

"We're going to sit down now. Daddy called him and asked him to come. If you have a problem with that, I'll throw your sorry ass out in the parking lot with the rest of the trash," I told her, and she flinched. "He's here, he's staying, and he's coming to the reception at the house. Momma wanted it. Daddy wants it. I want it. Got it?" The icicles became stones.

She recovered from her shock at me talking to her like that and narrowed her eyes. But she wisely moved aside and turned to talk with Patty, who was watching the exchange with interest and not a little amusement. Good fucking choice.

"Mark," Brian whispered as we took our seats, "I promise I didn't mean to start anything. I'll say something to your dad and slip out the back."

"Is *he* with you?" I asked. The icicles were back, for him now.

He hesitated. *Now* I could read him. I saw him clearly now that the scales had permanently fallen from my eyes.

"Mark, we aren't together. It only lasted about a month. I'm back here in town. I've got a small apartment, and I'm back at my old job. I knew you didn't want to hear from me, so I just... I didn't...." Part of me was celebrating. I hoped it fucking hurt, burned his ass like he did mine. But he'd only been with Henry or Harvey or whatever-the-fuck-his-name-was for a few months, not like a ten-year friendship turned love. Part of me was sad for him, because I didn't want him hurting. But the biggest part, right that minute, wasn't really there, was checked out and would weigh in after I buried Mom.

"Don't worry about it. We'll talk after the graveside service. And you *will* come to Daddy's afterwards. We can talk more then. Don't even think about ducking out, boy. 'Cause you *know* what'll happen if I have to come looking for you." I turned my head slightly sideways and gave him a flat look.

I thought I felt a little shudder. "Okay."

Just that. Okay. I relaxed and focused on the business at hand. The redneck preacher from East Bumfuck Egypt started the service, and I buried my momma.

CHAPTER FOUR

August 2001

"WHAT time will you be home?" he asked. This was the night I'd set aside every two weeks to have a massage. Brian knew it, but asked the same damn thing every two weeks. It made my head ache.

"I'll be home late. You know that. I'm having a massage tonight. I'll be there by midnight, so if you want to come over, just go on to bed. No need for you to wait up," I told him. I really didn't have the energy to get into an argument about it.

"But, it's your birthday. I thought...."

"I know it is. And this's my treat to myself. You and I're going out on Saturday, and we'll celebrate it then. Brian, we've been over this already. I need to get back to work. Is there something you needed?" If we hadn't talked about this shit three times this week already, I'd have probably been less of an ass about it.

But since we got back together, or at least were doing *something* together, he was very possessive of my time. Pretty fucking ironic when I thought about it, since he was the one cheating before and hiding crap.

He sighed. "No, I'll see you tonight. Love you."

And there it was.

"See you tonight then. Eat something, and I'll be there later. Bye," I mumbled.

I don't know why I couldn't say it back to him. Too much water under the bridge maybe? But if that was the case, why did I start things back up again? I sat back in my chair and looked up at the clock. Five o'clock was only a few minutes away. Yes, it was my birthday, and yes, I was thirty today, and yes, that was supposed to be some stinking big deal.

Twenty-nine was a big deal. Forty'll be a big deal. Thirty—just a blip on the radar.

I was supposed to meet Antonio for dinner, and then he was going to give me a massage as a present. Part of me wasn't sure why I didn't tell Brian about that, but to be honest, I was probably being a little chickenshit. Because, yes, I'd been hiding my friendship with Antonio from Brian.

At first, it was because I wasn't sure we *were* friends. Conversations before and after a massage I was paying for didn't constitute a close personal relationship to me by any stretch of the imagination. But after the funeral, it was… weird. On the one hand, I was getting closer to Brian again, and the times I saw him were good, but I still couldn't trust the man. Not fully. But then, Antonio called me out of the blue about two weeks after Brian and I started up again and asked me to go to lunch.

I wasn't sure how to handle that new development. Antonio said he was just checking in with me when he called, since I hadn't been by to see him in over a month. He knew things with Mom were close to an end because of the phone calls I got the last time I was there. I filled him in, and he asked me to go with him to lunch at Marie's. I was back at work, of course, but not really feeling right in my skin yet.

But something changed that day, sitting there eating pizza. After the mandatory *How is your day going, How was the funeral, I'm so sorry for your loss* stuff, he started talking about computers. Like nothing else was going on, like this was normal. And somewhere in the middle of that conversation, I found myself laughing and talking about shit I only knew a little about, and I saw Antonio a little differently.

He took the time to make me feel better. Treated me like a friend, showed me he cared. And my skin felt a little more normal again. Damn.

Since then, once every few weeks, I'd get a call and hear that big booming voice of his. "Get your ass down to Marie's and have lunch with me. No fucking excuses. You have to eat. Get here now," and he'd hang up. I'd drop what I was doing and go. I never told anybody about it. Not Brian, not Patty.

At the same time, I was seeing Brian a couple of times a week. At first, it was just a phone call to see if I was okay. Then I was calling him to check in. We had lunch a few times. Then dinner.

It was three months before I'd taken him to bed again.

WE WERE sitting at The Colonnade. It was a Saturday night, so of course the place was packed. At least we'd gotten there ahead of the worst of it and were seated so we could watch the procession.

The Colonnade was a landmark in Atlanta. Blue-haired ladies sat side by side with all the Midtown gay boys. The food was wonderful— what's not to like about fried chicken, and yeast rolls and beef stroganoff made from scratch? But the crowd, that was why we were there. It rivaled anything on *Golden Girls* or *Designing Women*.

The last time Brian and I'd been there for dinner, there was a table of twinks and their mothers next to us. We'd just been seated. It was the middle of summer, and Atlanta in August—no fucking picnic. Anyway, this darling little blond boy looked at his mother as he fanned himself with the menu and said, "I have just been moist *all* day."

Yeah, it's that kind of place.

So Brian and I were back there again, sharing that story and I was laughing and he was laughing. I looked at him and it hit me. I still loved him. Was *in* love with him.

Mother. Fucker. I didn't *want* to love him, because he'd hurt me, and I saw him in bed with that greasy piece of crap and how could he do that to me? But goddammit, I did. I could see it in his eyes when he realized what I was thinking, and his expression softened. His laugh faded.

"I'm so sorry." His eyes were so sad and my heart gave a lurch in my chest.

I sat there and realized this could go one of two ways. I could stay hard like stone, because that's what he deserved and I was a hard-ass. Or I could maybe try to feel a little of what made my mom call him, and remember that she loved him enough to do that after what he did to me. Remember that there must have been something more to him.

She'd adored him from the moment I brought him home the first time. Especially when she found out he didn't have any family. "Son, his mother *left* him? That bitch," she cried.

After that, she insisted he come over at least once a week to have dinner. When the two of us finally got together, I think she was happier than we were. She just wanted him to be loved. And she'd call him to make sure he was okay and eating enough. She called him her adopted son. She and Dad had even taken the training to become foster parents for kids needing emergency placements so that boys and girls who were scared and hurting would have a good, safe home when they were first put into care. All because of what she'd seen Brian go through. She loved him that much.

She wanted him in her life. In mine.

This is what a leap of faith feels like, I thought. I reached out and wiped away a tear that ran down his cheek and patted his jaw.

After dinner was over, we drove back to my house. The dogs were ecstatic to see him again, and that felt right too. He petted them and loved on them and accepted wet, sloppy dog licks on the mouth and scratched their bellies. They went into the den with the pet gate up and he went into my bedroom.

"Mark, I want you to know—" he got out before I pushed him against the door and took over his mouth with mine. I ground against him, held his head between my hands, and kissed him hard. I brought all the anger, the grief, the passion, the hate, and most of all the love I still felt for this man into that kiss.

He went still and let me take him. Make no mistake, he fucking kissed me back like he was as hungry for it as I was, but he knew I had all the control here, and he let me have it. It was just what I needed and what I craved from him. If we were going to do this, it was damned well going to be *my* way and at *my* pace.

It was March in the city, so the nights were still cool. Brian was in jeans and a sweater I'd given him for Christmas a couple of years before. It was this creamy silver color that looked so good with his bright blue eyes. I was not really the romantic sort, but I liked to see my guy dressed nice. And he was a fine-looking man, even if he was no longer mine. After tonight, he was going to be mine again.

I moved far enough away that I could run my hands up under his sweater to feel his chest. He wore an undershirt to keep his nipple rings from catching in the weave of the sweater, but that just made me rougher with my groping. My hands ran across his smooth pecs and grabbed, pinched nipples and tugged the rings and swallowed his moans into my mouth. I never let that sweet mouth go.

His sweater went up and over his head, forcing me to let his mouth go for a moment. He looked into my eyes and I saw uncertainty. He wanted me, but I knew he didn't know what this meant. I did though, and went about showing him.

I pulled his T-shirt up and off, reaching with my mouth to grab a nipple. My teeth caught it, and I tugged and bit and worked the ring. The sounds he made went straight to my cock. He never asked for mercy or begged for more or less, he just groaned and sucked in air. It made my cock hard and uncomfortable in my pants.

I pinched his other nipple with one hand, still sucking the other bud. My other hand snaked behind him to grope that ass. So firm, so tight, it was beautiful. I slid my hand into the waistband and felt nothing but skin. Commando—the fucker knew what that did to me. My fingers went deeper, ran down the crease of his ass, rubbed the smoothness, and teased right over his hole.

That made him move against me, broke the control he held onto so tightly. He tried to push back to get some friction against my fingers, but I took my hand out of his jeans and pulled up and away from him. This time all I saw in his eyes was need. And I knew what he wanted.

"Get those jeans off if you want me to fuck you," I whispered. I didn't trust my ability to speak above that—I might have yelled or growled or let something into my voice I didn't want him to hear yet.

I moved to the bathroom and grabbed the bottle of lube and a condom. We used to go bare, but I didn't know what he'd done and with whom. So, no glove, no love. And honestly, I heard all that shit about the sensitivity, blah, blah, blah, but my cock never knew the difference between skin and raincoat, because, really, it loved ass regardless.

When I turned back around, he was naked. I took a moment to appreciate the man in front of me. He was my age, jet-black hair and eyes blue like the sky. Shorter than me by three inches or so. Solid, like a gymnast, but not ripped, just… right. Smooth and pale. Pierced nipples that were nice and swollen from my mouth and fingers. He stood still, bare-assed and waiting.

"Get on the bed. On your back. I want to watch this," I ordered.

He looked at me for a minute, and then lay on his back crossways on the bed. He pulled his knees up, rested his feet flat on the bed, hands to his sides. He knew how to turn me on. His submission always did.

I rounded the foot of the bed and undressed slowly, not looking at him at all. That's what cranked his engine—the waiting, the anticipation of knowing I *was* going to take him, but not *when*. So I drew it out, tucked my socks into my sneakers, folded my jeans just so. Then picked the lube and rubber up and tossed them on the mattress beside him and edged around the side.

He could only look up, seeing me framed between his bent knees. I grabbed his thighs and pulled him to me, so his ass rested right at my crotch level. My hard cock brushed against his spread cheeks, and I saw him jump a little. His cock flopped up against his lower stomach. He wanted this as much as I did.

"How many?" I asked. He looked at me before answering. Both of us knew what I meant.

"Just him. I promise, I swear on whatever you want me to swear on. It was just him." His voice was steady and he met my eyes without blinking. Funny, I believed him.

"He's gone?" I had to know.

"Yes, he's gone. I never wanted him, really. He's gone," he swore.

"We won't talk about him again. If I do this, you don't fucking spread your legs for anybody else. This's your one last chance, Brian. There won't be another. Do you understand me?"

No hesitation from him. "I understand. I don't want anyone else. I'm yours."

I didn't answer with words. Instead, I reached beside him and grabbed the condom. After tearing the package open, I rolled it down my length, making sure it was tight. Then I popped open the lube and ran a thin stream of it over my cock.

"Don't come until I say so." I slicked up my shaft.

"I remember," he whispered, his breath shallow and fast. He knew what was coming and he looked ready to shoot now.

I grabbed him behind his knees and pushed them back, his feet against the flat of my chest. I positioned my cock against his hole and rested it there. Looking him in the eye, I tugged his hips hard toward me and shoved inside.

He tensed, then relaxed, opening himself to me and welcoming me inside him. I saw the struggle on his face.

I took him this way when I knew he needed it hard and fast. Hardly any lube, just making him take me. That sharp burst of sensation always made him "be present." His words, not mine. I could see his breath as it began to even out. I pulled out and slammed back in, taking the pace hard and fast right from the get-go. He would always adjust, and he did now. He was so fucking tight, but he opened enough to take it.

He kept his hands to the sides like he always did. His legs spread open wide, my hard cock pounding in and out of him, he looked so fucking beautiful. I kept up a hard pace, knowing I wouldn't last long. It'd been way too long, and I needed to come inside him so badly. I could see the sweat starting to pop up on his brow—he needed this too.

I shifted a little and could tell when I hit his prostate. His cock started to swell, then leak, and I saw his mouth working, his jaw clenching and relaxing. I held his thighs in a vise grip and managed to gasp, "Work those nipples for me."

His gaze locked on mine. His hands relaxed the death grip they had on the comforter and pulled and twisted the hoops. I had to close my eyes for a moment; the way his ass tightened around my cock almost made me blow my load right then.

I kept this up for a minute or two but I felt the pressure start building in my balls and spine. I knew it would all be over with soon. "Come for me. Now. Or you fucking don't get to," I growled out at him.

He looked me square in the eyes, tugged the rings hard as hell, and shot all over his chest.

And that was all she wrote. I pushed in maybe three more times and lost my load. His insides spasmed around me while my orgasm ripped its way out. My knees gave out and I flopped down on him, forcing his legs wide apart, making him take my weight for a minute while I caught my breath.

When I got some strength back, I stood and walked over to the bathroom. "Stay," I ordered.

I tugged off the condom and threw it in the toilet, stopping to take a piss while I did. After I flushed, I grabbed a washcloth and waited while the water warmed, then went over to him. He lay there like I left him, sweat and globs of cum dotting him from chest to groin. Debauched. I cleaned him off and looked away, smiling.

"Move your ass over and let's get some rest," I told him, and reached for the lamp.

THAT was five months ago, and while we weren't living together again, we were seeing each other exclusively.

Here I was on my birthday, having dinner with my massage therapist, who was fast becoming a really good friend. And evidently still totally straight, because there was some woman sitting there with her hands all over him when I got to the table.

I thought I looked totally dignified as I called his name and waited until he turned his attention from her skanky ass to me.

"Hey, dude, happy birthday. This is Rianna. She's Mario's sister—you know, my buddy from back home. She's in town taking a break from the husband and kids and staying with me a few days," he explained.

What. The. Fuck. I seemed to think this a lot where Antonio was concerned.

"Well, nice to meet you, Rianna. Maybe we should do this another time, Antonio," I mustered.

"Nah," he laughed. "She's gonna go out dancing and have a good time and we'll have our time together. Right, honey?"

"Right, baby," the mass of Lee Press-on Nails and weave said.

"Fantastic," I drawled.

"See you later, dollbaby." He grinned and gave her a wet, openmouthed kiss and a quick smack on the ass as she teetered away on heels three inches too high for a hooker.

That's when it hit me. I was fucking jealous.

Mother. Fucker.

CHAPTER FIVE

WE FINISHED dinner, and I let him carry the weight of the conversation. I was only half there anyway; all the thoughts spinning around in my head needed to settle the fuck down. I was *not* going to be attracted to a straight guy again. Every gay man out there has at least one man-crush in his past that totally shriveled his nads into raisins and sent him screaming off into the night. Or into the straight dude's fist. Mine ended in a lost friendship.

So I got my shit together right then and there. Antonio didn't seem to notice, and before I knew it I'd heard the whole sordid story of Rianna, her hot-headed Cuban husband, her "brats," and how she liked to just get away and let off steam every few months. Her brother Mario was an old friend of Antonio's, and evidently starred in some kind of adult films and did massage on the side.

But he was the happy ending kind of masseur. And also had a very nasty drug habit that reared its ugly head now and again. Antonio would sober him up, kick his ass, call his sister, and she'd come and take him home. Then the cycle would repeat. Rianna was out having a good time while Mario was sleeping it off before they went back home to Miami the next day.

And, oh yeah, she and Antonio were going to spend the night together. Wink, wink, nudge, nudge. Not my fucking concern.

After he paid the bill, I followed him back over to his apartment. My resolve was righteous—I'd get my massage and get back home. There was a guy who wanted my cock at home in my bed. That's where my focus needed to be, not on this beautiful disaster.

"Want some wine, birthday boy?" he asked. He already had the glasses out, ice in one. *Shudder*.

"Maybe just a half glass tonight, man. I'm kind of out of it already." I shrugged.

He poured our drinks and sat down beside me on the sofa. I noticed how close he sat, and my mind took off running again. Granted, he had the personal boundaries of a three-year-old sometimes, but he never did anything except sit there.

I was way too fucking aware of him. How he smelled. How the muscles in his arms flexed. Fuck.

"Maybe I should just make it an early night tonight, Antonio. Brian said he might come over, and I'm sure he wants to give me his present." I waggled my eyebrows.

He looked at me like I kicked his puppy. How in the fuck did a man like him manage to pout? "No, man. I got something special planned tonight. You can't bail on me now. Let me get things set up."

Well, fuck. I tried. And, really, I could use the massage. Maybe he could rub my brain and unknot all the shit racing around and bumping and pinging like a pinball machine. I watched him pull out the massage table, set it up, and drape it with sheets and towels.

He went over to the table where he had all his computer and stereo crap set up and clicked on the soft rock channel of an Internet radio station. Big pussy loved Barry Manilow, Gordon Lightfoot, Linda Ronstadt. All the good stuff. And damn it, I liked it too.

Jeffrey Osborne started crooning about flying away on the wings of love.

"Go ahead and get ready while I warm up the oil, baby."

Baby?

Oh yeah, that made me want to strip naked. No, really. It made me want to strip *naked*. So I did, and crawled up on the massage table and put my head in that little doughnut thingy.

I heard Antonio come back in the room, then felt the light touch of his hands and the warmth of the oil as he started rubbing circles right between my shoulder blades. He always targeted that area first—evidently I carried a lot of tension there. And it felt so wonderful, the pressure getting deeper and harder. I could feel the muscles relax. I took in a deep breath and settled down on the table.

Something felt… different. I couldn't place it but shrugged it off. Probably my imagination working overtime.

He moved around the table and stood near my head, working on my neck. It hit me then, I didn't feel his shirt brushing against me. He always wore those baggy T-shirts, two or three sizes too big, and I could feel them on my skin as he leaned in close to reach an area. And it wasn't there. I opened my eyes in shock, but since my head was in the round thingy, all I could see was the floor, and his bare feet. And bare calves.

He must have felt the sudden tension in my back and neck. "What's the matter, baby?" he asked.

Baby again.

"Antonio. Are you… naked?" I hoped my voice was even.

"Yeah. You're gonna massage me after I finish with you. I know you like what you see. Happy birthday," he murmured.

Fuck. That. Shit.

"I don't know the first thing about massaging somebody. And what do you mean I like what I see? We're buddies, aren't we? I know you aren't gay and, dude, this shit just ain't right." I knew I was rambling on like an idiot, and my accent got all country when I was nervous.

I didn't know how to say *bad idea*. Really *bad idea*.

Oh. Yeah. "Antonio, this is really a bad idea."

"Shhhh. It's a great fucking idea. I get tired and sore too and this way, I don't have to pay nobody. You get to feel my muscles and rub on my ass and then you go home and get laid, and I'm gonna fuck Rianna. Everybody wins," he crowed.

It had a strange logic to it. Looking wasn't cheating. Touching wasn't cheating, as long as I wasn't touching his ass with my dick. *That* was cheating. He got laid later, and I could go home and get me some too. And I was *so* not going to think about his ass and my dick together.

When he put it that way, yeah, everybody wins.

I settled back down and he worked on my aching neck and back. Once I allowed myself to relax and get over my concerns, it was just like every other massage he'd done for me since last year. The nice dinner and the glass of wine made me drowsy, and when I turned over for him to work on my front, I almost didn't open my eyes.

Yeah, almost. But I did. The lights were low, but I could see him, barely, through my slitted eyelids. The body I imagined didn't do him any justice at all. Almost six feet tall, he was built like a wrestler. I already knew he had really muscular arms from what he'd been doing to my body, and I'd wager he could crack walnuts in his hands. But the rest, just… damn.

His shoulders were nice and wide, and his frame narrowed down toward his hips. Not the classic V-shape, he was a little thicker than that through the waist, but that chest was a fucking work of art. Nice solid muscles, a good dusting of hair that ran the width of it, then down to his stomach and further.

I could see that the tattoos ran down his neck and splashed onto his chest and down his arms. It was too dark to make out the details, but the shadow of them on his skin was… eerie. As he moved around the edge of the table to work on my leg, I could see everything else.

Holy fuck. I'm not huge, but I'm not ashamed to walk around the locker room either. Yeah, I've been in a locker room and know my way around the gym, just not a bunny. His cock was long and thin and nicely shaped, and his balls hung big and full. He shaved down there, but then not everybody's perfect. And his thighs. Fuck, they were thick and muscled like a cyclist's.

But I saw that ass and didn't know if I could stay soft. It was fucking beautiful. Tight, chiseled, and round. Did I say tight? When he moved further up, massaging my thighs, I could see how smooth it was, and I had to think about awful things to keep my cock quiet. Like where he might bury me after strangling me with those strong hands when Mr. Happy stood up and spit in his eye. He might have touched me down there once, but it hadn't been on the table again since. So to speak.

He moved up and started working on my hip, using long strokes from waist to knee with both hands. His cock brushed against my right forearm as it lay on the edge of the table. I practiced my deep breathing and stared up at the ceiling. He didn't say a word, just kept massaging.

"How you feeling there, champ?" he asked.

"Doing good. Out of it. Back feels good. Needed this," I almost whispered.

"Good. Now get your ass up and we can switch places."

Oh God. Ohgodohgodohgod.

I eased off the table. He straightened the sheet and put a fresh towel on the head thing, and laid facedown.

"The oil's next to the computer," he said, his voice muffled through the hole. "Don't use much, a little goes a long way. Start on my neck, right between my shoulders, just like I do with you. You'll be fine."

I squirted a little of the oil on my hands and rubbed them to warm it up. It had the light smell of almonds and something like vanilla—I'd always liked the smell of it. I looked down on the feast spread out on the table and said a little prayer for strength and sanity. And put my hands on him.

I think I worried so much about screwing up that it took me a good fifteen or twenty minutes to even appreciate how good his body felt. He was hard as a fucking rock, but not skinny and lean like so many vain guys were. He had heft to him, and I appreciated it.

I worked the oil into his back and down his shoulders, massaging one side, then the other. I was careful to keep one hand touching him at all times; he'd explained that trick to me one time. It makes you feel grounded and connected and never alone. Nice feeling.

As I moved up to stand at the top of the table to rub the back of his neck and across his shoulders and arms, I let my gaze wander down his body and took it all in. It was really beautiful, if you can call a man that. I felt close to him, but somehow the energy was sensual but not... sexual. Erotic, yes, but I didn't want to fuck him. He looked totally relaxed, his breathing even and deep.

I moved around, down the side of the table and worked his back, arms, and down to his hands. He started moaning when I picked one up and squeezed hard. Now *that* got my attention.

"Oh, man, harder, tighter. That feels so good on my hands. Press as hard as you can," he panted out. Fuck, that made my cock twitch.

I grabbed his hand and worked it as hard as I could and really started to get into the noises he was making. I put it down and started on his lower back and hips. And that amazing ass. I oiled up my hands, then rubbed and groped and squeezed and spread those glutes and ran my fingers down the crack. My knuckles brushed against his balls and my cock twitched a little again.

I stroked down his legs and worked those muscles with long, strong strokes. Moving around to the bottom of the table, I picked up one foot, then the other, all the time looking up at his ass. I worked my way back up the other side and ended up back at his shoulders.

I coughed a little. "Turn over," I managed to rasp out.

He flipped over and settled back down, his eyes closed. I didn't know where to start, so I squirted some oil on his chest. It must have been cold because he jumped a little. I rubbed it in and was careful not to touch his nipples. They crinkled, but I ignored them.

I was able to make out more details of the tattoos that decorated him. There were Japanese letters and symbols running down his neck, ending on both forearms. The word "Jason" was in delicate blood red lettering across the left part of his chest. There was a small handprint on his right pec, in the same red ink. I ran my fingers across it, outlining the fingers.

"Jason's handprint when he was one year old," he murmured without opening his eyes.

I moved my hands across his stomach to his hips and down his thighs. That heavy one-eyed snake stared at me but lay there quietly. Thank God.

When I got to his feet, I patted the sole of his foot. "All done. Get your lazy ass up."

He stood up and we faced each other for a long moment. "Happy birthday, baby." He wrapped me in a bear hug and kissed me right on the mouth.

When I got home, I woke Brian up by fucking him, as they say, right through the mattress.

CHAPTER SIX

May 2002

I PULLED into the parking lot at the City Athletic Club at six in the morning. I really, really hated that time. But in order to get in any kind of workout, I had to get to the gym that early. My office hours started at nine, and this was the closest club with a heated pool that I could find. An hour of cardio, some weight training, maybe a little basketball, and then finish in the steam room. A quick shower and I'd be ready for work.

Antonio met me here a couple of times a week and was coaching me on my workout routine. I had absolutely no inclination to be a muscle god. Hell, I couldn't if I tried, but keeping that extra couple of inches off my waist was worth it. That and it allowed me to eat pasta and pizza and mu shu shrimp. And beer and wings.

"Good morning, Mr. Jennings. How are you today?" the perky little piece at the reception desk asked. I didn't do coffee, but I was seriously considering it so I could deal with Little Mary Sunshine four mornings a week.

"Fabulous. It's 6:00 a.m. and my bed's calling me. Maaaark, come baaaaack," I deadpanned.

A bright Stepford smile greeted me. It was *so* not going to be my day. "Antonio's here already and asked me to tell you he would be on the basketball court," she chirped. I swear.

"Thanks," I said, moving off away from her and her fucking rainbows and unicorns. I went to the locker room and put my clothes and toiletries away, and grabbed a couple of towels. If we were going to be on the court, I knew it'd be a sweaty morning.

There he was, baggy shirt, fatigues, and Doc Martens. The man never paid attention to the signs saying "Sneakers Only," and nobody had the balls to say anything to him. Although I do think Mary Poppins tried once. He probably fucked her to get his way because she never brought it back up.

"Jennings, get your ass in here, boy. Where you been?" he yelled. Thank God we were the only two on the courts that time of morning, because he had absolutely no shame.

He tossed the ball to me, and I started dribbling down the court slowly. It was too early and I wasn't warmed up enough to do much serious running. So I took a shot at the goal and it went in.

"The king, the undisputed ruler of the universe," I chuckled and did a little fist pump and dance.

"Shut the fuck up and get your ass in gear," he shouted, passing me the ball again.

I made that bucket, too, then did a little reprise of the dance. My blood started to flow and I woke up a little more. I could see the dark circles under his eyes and the clenched jaw. The yelling and trash talk was just a front, I'd learned. This was how he got when something was on his mind. Sure enough, Antonio started yelling. "Move that tired old ass, man," he threw at me as he ran down the court in front of me. I sped up and went in for a layup that rolled around the rim before falling out. Antonio grabbed it and sprinted down the lane, dribbling the ball so hard I expected it to bounce away.

We'd been friends for long enough now for me to pick up on his moods a little better. Whatever it was, he'd either tell me or he wouldn't. I wasn't going to try to drag it out of him, because then he got really pissy, and fuck *that* noise. "Put up or shut up, Hetboy. Looks like I'm up by four already, and all that's really running is your mouth." He turned, glared at me, and took a shot for three. It went in, and a flicker of a smile started to show on his lips as he grabbed his crotch and tilted his head at me. "Fuck you," he growled and took off down the court again.

We played in silence for about another twenty minutes after that, and then the pace started to slow down. "Let's take a break and go sit in the sauna. I could really use the heat, man," he grumbled.

He headed to the locker room, and we stripped down, put on our towels, and headed into the hot room. I was used to him being naked around me now and didn't really bother to steal glances. I flat out looked. He always strutted a little when he noticed. The boy liked being looked at, and I didn't want to disappoint him.

We settled down, and I poured a ladle of water on the hot grill, making the steam rise up. The quiet time and the steam room were my treats to myself after a hard workout or a bad night. The heat seemed to draw all the tension out of my system, leaving me feeling drained and empty but good.

"I need to ask you a favor. I fucking hate to do it, and you can say no and I won't hold it against you, but I really, really need you to help me," he blurted.

Shit. This must be a doozy if he was this worked up over asking me to help him out with something. "What do you need? You know if I can, I will," I told him. And I meant it.

He sat there, looking down at his boots and not saying anything. I stayed quiet and waited it out. A man had to have his pride.

"I'm behind two months on my child support. Jeanine's threatening to not let me see Jason until I get caught up. Things've been better with her, but she's only working part-time and needs the money. Business hasn't been good the past couple of months, and I just don't have it," he admitted quietly.

He looked up into my eyes, and what I saw there hurt me. His face looked so scared and resigned.

"I need to borrow some money. I promise you I'll pay it back. We can sign a note and make installments or whatever. I just can't not see my son." His voice cracked. To see this rock of a man broken over not seeing his little boy, it would have taken a better man than me not to be moved.

"I can lend it to you. How much do you need?" I asked.

"Fourteen hundred dollars." He looked down and winced.

Well, shit. It wasn't like I didn't have it, but it was in my savings account. I used a credit union, and I'd have to go there to withdraw the funds. But the bigger concern to me was loaning money to a friend. The quickest way to fuck up a relationship with a friend or family member was to loan them money. Been there. Done that.

You know, the general rule of thumb is don't loan money you know you won't see again.

"How about this?" I thought out loud. "I'll loan you the money, but every time I get a massage, we'll deduct that much from the balance 'til it's paid off. We can put it in writing, so we're both covered, and that way we both feel better about it."

"Thanks, man." The relief in his eyes plain. "Let's go take a shower and get some breakfast. Can we write it up and do it today?" There was hope on his face now, some of that tension released.

"Yeah, but you owe me some damn mighty fine massages. Double massages. Triple! You got to grow four more hands," I joked to lighten the mood. He looked at me and laughed.

"I can arrange for another guy to come over and give you a four hand massage. Or you can bring your man and I can do you both," he offered, more like himself again.

As if.

Brian didn't like anybody touching him. Those years he'd spent in foster care had damaged him in ways that hurt me to see. Made me want to track down some of those motherfuckers who posed as caring, giving foster parents and beat them bloody. So, no, he wouldn't be joining me.

We'd gotten back together, and he was living with me again. It was good. I loved him. I just wish he could forgive himself, because I had. As hard as it'd been, I'd made my peace with what happened and tried to show him with my words and my actions that I still loved him and wanted him.

But there was just something… broken about him. He'd look at me and flinch sometimes. His mood would change suddenly and he'd get quiet. I'd found myself treating him like he was a child almost, and that was fucking weird. But that just made him mad, and when he got mad he did stupid shit. Like lash out at me. Or not talk to me at all for days. Something just wasn't right.

I snapped out of wherever the hell my head went and looked at Antonio.

"No, Brian won't want to come. Maybe a four hand would be nice though. We can talk about it. And I'm buying breakfast, so you, my friend, are having the...," I started.

"Oh fuck no I'm not," he yelled, more like himself now.

"Rooty Tooty Fresh and Fruity breakfast. With smiley-face pancakes." I grinned. He hated ordering that.

"Real men don't eat that shit. Steak and eggs, man, not some fruity gay breakfast," he snorted and pushed me toward the locker room.

"Ah, but I am gay, grasshopper." I nodded wisely, bowing.

"You just ain't met the right woman yet." He whipped his towel off, bending over to get his clothes out of the locker.

"And you haven't met the right man. Or maybe you have." I smiled evilly and leered at his ass.

He softened and looked at me. "Oh, yeah, I met the right man, all right. A fucking miracle. An angel here on earth." His voice was soft as cotton and his eyes shone like diamonds.

What could I say to that?

I TOOK a long lunch break and went by the credit union to get the cash Antonio needed. Given that he was having such a rough go of it, I went ahead and withdrew an even two thousand dollars. One thing about the way I was raised, my mom always taught me to share as long as I had something. Good things come back to you and all that, she'd said.

God, I still missed her so much. And I really wanted him to be okay.

We met up right after work, before I headed home. It felt like one of those hit-and-run things, or a drug deal. We arranged to meet in the parking lot of the grocery store halfway between my office and his apartment. When I got out and walked over to his truck, I saw he wasn't alone. Sitting in the passenger seat was a small person. A boy. Oh hell, it must be Jason.

"Hey man, I got a surprise for you," Antonio said, the excitement loud and clear in his voice and his face was animated again. He jumped out of the truck and went around to the passenger side. He unbuckled the kid and they both came around the front.

I had *puh-lenty* of nephews and nieces, so I could tell he was about ten. He looked like a little chip off the big cannoli. Strong features, dirty blond hair. Big-ass smile and he walked like he owned the world. I liked him immediately. He walked right up to me and stuck out his hand.

"Hi. You must be Mark. My name's Jason. Dad said I'd get to meet a friend of his today." He eyed me up and down, and that kind of appraisal from a kid was amusing. It was really easy to tell he was his dad's son. "He's been looking for a new friend since Mario went back home. So, do you have any kids? Is that your car? It's nice, but I like my dad's truck better. I can see out the windows but they're tinted so we can watch everybody else and nobody can see us." I swear it felt like a ten-year-old's version of a police interrogation.

"It's good to meet you, Jason." I smiled and shook his hand. "Yes, I'm a friend of your dad's. No, I don't have any kids. And yes, that's my car." I laughed, looking up at Antonio.

The pride in his eyes was fucking amazing. It was good to see him smiling and happy after this morning. It was kind of weird to see him like this though—as Dad. Usually he was so blustery and macho and imposing. Or tried to be anyway—I wasn't anybody's bitch. But to see him like this, this was new. And I liked it.

"Why don't you jump back in the truck and we'll go and get some dinner in a minute, buddy. Okay?" he told his boy.

Jason climbed back in through his dad's side of the truck after giving me one more glance, and Antonio closed the door. I came up beside him and we stood there, side by side with our backs leaned against the cab. I figured I needed to be a little discreet here, so I pulled out the envelope and reached over and slid it in his front pants pocket.

"Here," I explained, "we can talk about the details later. The paper for you to sign's in there. I'll get it from you tomorrow at the gym. Go have dinner with your kid. I need to get going."

"You can come with us if you want to. Jason usually wants hamburgers or chicken fingers. But I make him eat healthier stuff and we might go to the sushi place over on Piedmont," he said, looking kind of hopeful.

"I can't. Brian and I have plans tonight. We're having dinner with my dad."

He looked down, frowned a little, and then back up at me. His gaze met mine for a minute and I wasn't sure exactly what I saw there. It wasn't bad, just like he had something he wanted to say but didn't quite know how, or what. Then it was gone.

"Cool. You guys have a good night," he said quietly.

He stuck out his hand, and I looked down at it. We never shook hands. I reached out, took it and gave it a firm shake. It went on for maybe three seconds longer than it should have. Then he pulled me into a man hug, bumping shoulders, and let me go with a squeeze. He climbed up in that fucking ridiculous huge truck thing, buckled himself and Jason up, then left.

If I didn't know better, I would think he was compensating for something with that monstrosity. Hah. But I did know better.

CHAPTER SEVEN

December 2002

CHRISTMAS in my family always meant family dinner at Dad's on the Sunday before the actual holiday. It started out that way so that each of us siblings could spend Christmas Day with our own spouses and kids, and any single sibs could catch a fucking break from the noise of early rising, over-sugared kids. Now, though, we all had someone. I loved my nieces and nephews, but I was more than ready for them to go back home after about two hours of playing, screaming, and fighting.

Last year was the first one without Mom, and we all managed to make it the whole meal without crying. She'd loved the holidays so much, and it felt like a hole in my heart the whole time I sat there and looked at her empty chair. Nobody could sit there. And Dad glanced at it every ten seconds so sadly.

I couldn't take it again, so this year I went over early and Brian and I decorated a tree. Put up all the lights and even wrapped garland and fairy lights around her chair. I tried to put the reindeer out on the front lawn, one on top of the other like they were humping, but Dad took them down and said Mom would've kicked our asses.

While the holidays weren't what they used to be, we were at least able to celebrate again without having to feel like it was forced.

And damn, but the kids loved it. Brian'd called each one of my brothers and sisters and gotten favorite toy names, clothes sizes, and video game preferences. He took this huge-ass list and the Jeep out to the malls and came back late Friday night with more presents than I'd seen. Ever. We'd stayed up late that night, then again on Saturday wrapping and tagging everything.

Brian was an only child. He'd never gotten close to any of the foster families he was with as a teenager, and of course the Egg and Sperm Donors, as he called his parents, were God only knows where. Fuck 'em.

Every year, on Christmas and his birthday, I swore if I ever found them, I'd kill them. He didn't know I saw him go into the bathroom every fucking year on those days and that I heard the sobs from the shower. That grief was his alone; it would have been unwelcome and an invasion for me to betray his dignity by bringing it out into the light. But someday, I thought, someday I hope I run into those fuckers and then they would know.

And that's why I let him do anything he wanted with my family. The kids adored him. He'd get down in the floor and play Hot Wheels, or Barbie, or GI Joe, and was always friendly to all of my brothers and sisters. Even the Holy Roller, the Asshole, and Sister Mary Vagina.

My sister Linda was the Holy Roller. She was the one who was ashamed to let her preacher know she had a gay brother. She and her husband Roy had a boy and a girl. She didn't know it, but he'd made a pass at my sister Patty while Linda was in the hospital giving birth to their daughter. One of our little family secrets we all knew but never talked about.

Sam was the Asshole. He was a former Marine and just fucking pleased as punch he had a faggot for a brother. And wasn't above telling anybody who would listen that he hated how Mom and Dad called Brian their adopted son. He never quite managed to say it loud enough for Dad to hear. He was fifteen years older than me, and when I met one of his future girlfriends for the first time when I was a toddler, I threw my bottle at her and broke her nose. Even then I knew how to make a statement. He and his alcoholic wife Jean had a daughter.

Brenda was Sister Mary Vagina. She had three marriages under her belt, and the first one of her exes was now gayer than me. He had this little white streak in the front of his hair that everybody said was from when he got really sick as a young man. Bullshit. Peroxide sickness if I knew him. Her present husband Frank, who I actually kind of liked, had gone to high school with my mother.

Yeah.

They went to church three times a week and she prayed for me and Brian every time they went, she was sure to tell me. She had three children: a son and daughter by her first husband—the Twink—and a son by the third. Those kids especially loved Brian and would go to him when nobody else could calm them down.

Patty and her husband Ray had two kids, both boys. Ray was a good guy, and if he wasn't straight I would have had him on his back with his legs in the air so fast he wouldn't know what hit him. He was six-two, one hundred eighty pounds of hairy hunk. If he lived in Wyoming he would've been a cowboy. Brian and I both always walked behind him so we could watch his ass. And those long legs with the slight bow. Usually Patty was right there with us. Also usually whispering, "Mine, all mine" in my ear. Bitch.

Robert was my younger brother. He was newly married but had two kids, both girls by two women other than his wife. But he and I were the closest in age and got along well enough. He was a dreamer and wanted to be a writer. He wrote poetry that was beautiful, but it didn't pay the bills. His wife Jennifer was a social worker and made most of the money in the family. She was a little wisp of a woman but I wouldn't want to fuck with her. I'd fear for my balls.

So there were the six of us sibs, plus spouses and kids. And I counted Brian as a spouse, significant other, whatever the fuck. And with Dad, that made twenty-three for dinner. And twenty-one people we bought presents for. More love and fun and fussing and wrapping paper than you could shake a stick at.

Antonio had repaid the money he borrowed in cash. He didn't want to work it out in trade, so I let him give me money as he got it. Since it was a pain in the ass to go to the credit union, I'd stuck it in a drawer and forgot about it. When it came time to shop, I just handed the wad of cash to Brian and told him to go forth and spend.

I sat back and watched as Brian took two of Brenda's kids and played Santa and they were his elves. They darted back and forth, distributing presents and gift bags and cards. I caught Brian's eye and gave him a smile, then put a little heat into it. He blushed a little, because he knew what *that* meant, and glanced away fast.

When I looked around, I saw Sam looking like somebody farted in his drink. He glared at me, and I mouthed "Fuck you" at him and gave him a middle finger salute. If he had his way Brian wouldn't be there. Hell, I wouldn't be either. No love lost.

But as Patrick Swayze says, nobody puts Baby in a corner. So I got up, reached in my pocket, and pulled out a hammered silver chain, like a collar, that I'd been carrying for just the right moment and came up behind Brian. I reached around and draped it across his neck and did up the clasp. He looked down, then around and up at me. His smile made me a little weak. Must be getting warm in here, I thought.

I turned him around and pulled him up against my chest and wrapped him in my arms. We were standing right there in front of the tree, my family, and God and I kissed him. Not a friendly kiss, or a brotherly kiss, or even a full-press fuck-me kiss. But it was long and deep and open eyed and it meant *I love you. Merry Christmas. You're mine.*

"Ewwww, they're kissing. Gross. Uncle Brian, stop, you're gonna get cooties," one of the rug rats screamed and tried to work in between us.

"Make him stop, Uncle Brian. I want you to play Legos with me. You said you'd play Legos with me, and you can kiss him and all that gross stuff when you go back to your house. Pleeeeaaaassseee, Uncle Brian," another one begged.

Brian grinned at them and pushed me back and said, "Okay, babies, just for you. Jed, you and Andrew get the boxes and we'll take them and put them on the table in the den, okay?"

That seemed to appease the little heathens. They grabbed a couple of their cousins and took off to get the boxes. He looked over his shoulder and raised his eyebrows at me. "Later," he promised, fingering his chain.

I smacked him on the ass and walked back into the dining room to get some more of the pecan pie I knew Patty'd made. She'd gotten the family recipe book after Mom died and was taking over as the baker in the family. Good damn thing, because none of us could make a decent crust except her.

"Fucking filthy faggots," my brother breathed as I passed by.

I stopped and leaned down so he could hear me, but nobody else could. I kept my voice low and looked straight ahead, a small smile on my face. Anybody looking would've thought I was sharing a quiet laugh with him. Well, maybe Brian would've known better.

"If you say one more fucking word, if you *use* that fucking word one more time, under your breath, out loud, however the fuck you want to do it, I'll knock you on your damn stupid redneck ass. Right the fuck out. You're nothing but a piece of shit. I'll call Child Protective Services and tell them how you kick Jean's ass when you have too much booze. And I *will* tell Dad too. Everything. Now are you going to shut your hateful mouth or am I going to shut it for you?" I asked, my voice quiet and even and low.

He went still and looked up at me. His eyes widened then narrowed and he started to open his mouth, but I wasn't done. Not yet.

"Think really, really hard about what you're going to say here. Because this is it. I'm done. You don't scare me and you never have. I let it go without saying anything because Dad loves you. I don't. It would hurt him if I kicked your worthless ass. I don't care anymore. Yes or no. Are you going. To shut. The fuck. Up?" I bit off every word, still smiling.

He didn't look at me. He just nodded and went back to his drink. I patted him on the shoulder, a little harder than necessary, and went off to look for that pie. God, that felt so fucking good.

LATER than night, at home, Brian and I sat on the couch watching television—one of my favorite traditions was a double feature of *A Charlie Brown Christmas* special and *How the Grinch Stole Christmas!*.

Mom had started that tradition. She'd fix us hot chocolate and we'd all sit and watch them every time they came on. I think I had both shows memorized by the time I was ten. Mom started buying me everything Grinch. I still had all of it in a box in my closet.

We each had a glass of wine and were cuddled up. For warmth. It was cold outside. And the blanket went further when we sat together.

"So you going to tell me what he said to you?" he asked. Linus was reciting what Christmas was all about.

"And lo, the angel of the Lord came upon them, and the glory of the Lord shone round about them, and they were sore afraid. And the angel said unto them, 'Fear not, for behold, I bring you tidings of great joy which will be to all people.'"

I considered bluffing. But he knew Sam and he knew something had passed between the two of us. And we were done lying and telling half-truths and pretending.

"He called us filthy fucking faggots one too many times. I called him a redneck wife-beating drunk for the first time. And I might have threatened to call CPS. And tell Dad. And kick his ass," I admitted.

"Good. I never said anything, but he came up to me at your mom's funeral and had some choice words for me. He doesn't matter so I never made a big deal out of it." He held my hand and rubbed circles on my palm. "But I love you for sticking up for me."

I was torn between anger and shock. The anger won out. Then I was so mad I almost couldn't get a good breath.

"What did he say?" I ground out.

"It doesn't—"

"Don't. What did he fucking say?"

A long moment went by. He stared at my hand while he rubbed it, deciding.

"He said if I ever cared a thing about your momma I'd get, and I quote, my fruity goddamn ass the fuck out of there and quit soiling the memory of his mother. Unquote. Oh, and he said it was a shame it wasn't me or you laid up in the casket instead of her. He also said something nice and hateful about how he hoped I got AIDS when I cheated on you, but that since we were fags I probably already had it since I let anything with a dick fuck me. He hoped you got it and died too," he admitted quietly.

"Well, just fuck him. No, fuck him twice and the mother fucking horse he rode in on and—"

I'd just gotten good and riled up when I felt Brian lay his head on my chest and put his arms around my stomach and just hug me, making shushing noises. I saw red, for God's sake, and the red I saw, I wanted it to be my brother's blood.

That, more than anything, brought me up short and back to myself. I wasn't a violent man. I stood there and took my lumps like a man and never hit anyone in anger, man or woman. And yeah, sometimes women deserved it just like a man did when they threw hate in your face. But I never went there. I just took it and swallowed it down and sweat it out like the poison it was.

I thought about it this time. I thought about it really hard.

"It's okay, babe. It's nothing we haven't heard before. And nothing we won't hear again. Maybe someday it won't be like that, but he doesn't matter," he kept saying. He kept it up and said anything that came to his mind as he talked me right down off the ledge.

"Merry Christmas, Charlie Brown! Hark, the herald angels sing, glory to the newborn king! Peace on Earth and mercy mild, God and sinners reconciled."

CHAPTER EIGHT

March 2003

I SAT in the middle of Chuck E. Cheese's and wondered what in the hell I was doing there. Around me, there must have been six thousand screaming kids all between six and twelve, all wanting to play with the same damn toys. Pizza, Coke (in the South we call all soda "Coke," deal with it) and birthday cake just served to energize all of them.

It was Jason's eleventh birthday and he demanded that his dad's best friend come too. When I tried to get out of it, Antonio handed the phone to him. I told him thirty-one was too old for Chuck E. Cheese's, and when his begging didn't work, threats of tears did. God, it would have been like kicking a puppy. And I couldn't do that. Yes, I'm an easy touch and a sucker. And he knew it. So here I sat, thanking God that at least there was beer in hell.

Antonio and I lounged there, watching Jason play with all his new friends. His mother had already thrown his regular birthday party at her house, and he's gotten his presents from all his cousins and friends. This day was to be something just for him and his dad. And now that included me.

Before the holidays, I'd gotten Jason a couple of small gifts and left them with Antonio under the small tree at his place. Evidently that was all it took for me to be part of Jason's family now. No "Uncle" stuff for him; I was just his dad's best friend and therefore expected to be there when he came over every other weekend. At the minimum I had to talk to Jason on his cell phone.

I still went for massages with Antonio, but somehow, after I loaned him the money and he paid me back, things changed. He didn't charge me for massage anymore, and we were better, closer friends now. He was forever thanking me for loaning him the money, and I finally ended up just nodding and patting him on the shoulder every time. But the Thursday night thing didn't change. We both ended up naked and massaging each other but it wasn't a business transaction. Not even friends with benefits.

I didn't tell Brian. He was okay with me getting the massages, and even with the two of us hanging out sometimes. I did what I wanted with my money and had my own friends and he did the same. We paid the joint bills, but I made a lot more than he did so I never worried about that kind of stuff. The mortgage was in my name but he wrote me a check every month for his part.

When he came back after my mom's funeral, Brian got his job as a courier for a medical supply company back. He didn't do well sitting eight hours at a desk, and didn't have much patience for bosses in his face. So the freedom to be out of the office and moving around was heaven for him, even in the total clusterfuck that was Atlanta traffic. He had no desire to do anything more at this point in his life, and it drove me crazy. I was always so worried something would happen while he was on the road.

But I knew he wouldn't understand two grown men who weren't fucking getting together and being naked. Even if one was straight. He could deal with me being naked—that was what happened with a massage. But Antonio being naked and me rubbing his body? I might be facing losing a couple of body parts I really, really enjoyed. He enjoyed them too, but he'd still cut them off while I slept.

And the thing was, it *was* totally innocent. Neither one of us got hard. There was no sex, no jerking off, nothing like that. But it was still an intimacy I didn't think I should share. It was private and nice, and not dirty. Still I kept it to myself.

So Antonio and I hung out, went to movies sometimes. I saw Jason about once a month. And now I was stuck at his birthday party, wishing I was anywhere in the world but there in the middle of all that noise. Damn it, why couldn't he have wanted to go to Manuel's Tavern?

"I appreciate you coming with us today. It means a lot to Jason," Antonio said, bringing me back to reality. Or at least this noisy, flashing version of it.

"I don't mind. Really. If he wants… this, then I can put up with it for an hour or two," I mumbled into my beer.

"I'll make it up to you. When I take him home, we can go back and hang out for a while. Have a couple of glasses of wine or something." He kind of looked sideways at me. Hopeful, it seemed like.

"Maybe. I really need to get home and do some things before Brian gets back. Saturday's laundry day and all that shit. Got to see about making some dinner too." What I didn't say, because I didn't want to make a big deal out of it, was that Brian had been having dizzy spells and passing out and I was trying to keep my eye on him. Until I could get his ass to the doctor anyway.

Antonio looked almost hurt. Disappointed.

"Isn't Rianna in town? I figured you guys would be hanging out? Mario's back too, isn't he?" I asked.

He leaned forward and dropped his voice so only I could hear him. "Yeah, she's in town. Mario's going to be staying with me for a little while so he can get back on his feet. This last time he started using was really rough. He was on the streets, and I think he might've been turning tricks. And Rianna, I'm not messing around with her anymore," he murmured, looking anywhere but at me.

I wasn't sure what to say. Mario was a nice enough guy when he was clean, but when he was using, he was a fucked-up bastard. He did massage too, and tried to talk me into using him instead of Antonio. He was a good-looking guy, olive-skinned and sleek and toned. But that was *so* not going to happen. He was Antonio's friend, but he was a user.

What was more curious was why Antonio wasn't fucking Rianna. I'd heard more than one story about the hot times the two of them had together. Her Cuban blood evidently made her a wildcat in bed. And I'd seen some of the scratch marks on Antonio's back from their last session. He'd even tried to get me to join in once.

I had to go back and explain the whole gay thing to him. Graphically. About how much I loved a hot ass. And body hair. Cocks and balls. All the things that made life worth living. His eyes had gotten big and round. Hell, if he wanted to tell me about his exploits, he was going to hear about mine. He didn't look disgusted, more like he saw me in a new light. Like he was trying to imagine what I was saying.

"Sooo, why aren't you and Rianna hooking up? You seeing somebody else? Been holding back on me?" I leaned in, wanting to know.

"Nah. Not exactly. I've just been busy and trying to make money. There's somebody I have my eye on, but I don't want to talk about it right now," he mumbled and wouldn't look at me.

What the hell was that about? Just then, Jason came over and started begging for more money for tokens. God, he was getting tall, I thought. All gangly arms and legs, and I could see he was going to be tall like his dad. I pulled out my wallet and gave him ten bucks. "Go get 'em, tiger," I told him. He took the money and gave me a grin, then ran before Antonio had a chance to say a word.

"Now tell me about this chick you're hung up on. What's the matter, you get shot down? That famous Italian charm on the fritz?" I teased.

He looked at me, and his face just kind of shut down. "No, it's nobody. No chick. Forget about it. You're spoiling Jason too much. He's gonna think you're an ATM. So what are you and Brian going to do later?"

"Well, we may go to a movie. Then home and hot monkey sex." I grinned and gave him the raised and waggling eyebrow thing.

He nodded and took at long drink of his beer. Didn't meet my eyes. Then looked out across the room and watched all the kids playing.

"Hey, buddy, are you okay? Something the matter? You can talk to me, you know. I'm a really good listener," I told him. This shit was beginning to worry me. He was never quiet like this unless…

Shit.

"Do you need some money? Is Jeanine threatening to not let you see Jason again? Because if that's the problem I can give you the money. Just tell me what—"

He interrupted me. "No, baby, I don't need any money. I'm okay. It's just been a long week and I probably need to just get some sleep. Just… forget about it."

He still wouldn't look at me. I just couldn't figure out why. But when he got in one of these moods, there was nothing to do except let him stew in it. I could feel his eyes on me when I wasn't looking, so I took a sip of my beer and looked out over the room. What was going on with him?

"So WHAT did you guys do today," Brian asked when we sat down to eat dinner.

"Took Jason to Chuck E. Cheese. Played soccer mom. Gouged my eyes out with a fork and stabbed my ears to stop the noise. Oh, the pain, Will Robinson, the pain…."

"Ah jeez, bet you were glad to get the heck out of there," he said.

"You have no idea. The weird thing is, I think there's something bothering Antonio. He wouldn't tell me, but there's something, I know it." I dished out the lasagna I made earlier.

"What do you think it is? What happened?" he asked, pouring out wine for us. "And damn, sweetheart, this all smells amazing."

"Thanks. But I don't know. Rianna's in town—you know, Mario's sister, the guy he grew up with—and they usually spend the weekend fucking up a storm. But he says they aren't this time, and kind of hinted he's interested in somebody," I told him while I dug in to dinner. "But he clammed up and wouldn't give me any details. I think he must have the hots for somebody that shot him down. Or...."

"What? What are you thinking?" he asked.

"I wonder if it's Jeanine. He hasn't mentioned anybody else. But the only other woman I know he sees is her. But hey, maybe he's just keeping it a secret for now. It's not like he tells me everything."

Brian looked thoughtful for a minute. "You think it could be a guy?"

I looked at him and stared for minute. He was serious. The thought surprised me, and made me uncomfortable for some reason. Actually, it made me a little pissed. "I don't think so. He doesn't set off my gaydar. He likes boobs too much. I never see him looking at other guys when we do anything. And he doesn't do *those* kinds of massages. No, I think it must be a woman," I stated firmly.

It damn well *better* be a woman. I thought and waited for a response, then looked up from my plate. I'd been focused on it because, damn, I made killer lasagna.

When I looked up Brian was shaking. His eyes were rolled back and I could see a little drool running out of the corner of his mouth. Then he dropped his fork and it hit the floor with a clang. Holy shit, he was having a seizure. Another one. My heart fell through my stomach and crushed my balls when it hit them, and the nausea and fear hit me like a fucking sledgehammer. I jammed it down, jumped up, and went around to his side of the table.

I grabbed my belt out from around my waist and doubled it over. I took his mouth and forced it open with pressure to both sides of his jaw and shoved the leather into his mouth to stop him from swallowing his tongue. Then I waited, made sure he didn't hurt himself. Watched over him and worried.

After about five minutes that felt like five hours, his seizure ended and his body relaxed. I picked him up and carried him into the den and laid him on the couch. His breathing evened out. His eyelids fluttered, and I could tell he was starting to come back around.

I stroked his face and talked silly nonsense to him to make the transition a little easier. And soon enough, his eyes opened and he struggled to focus on me. He tried to raise his head and get up, but I made him lay there. Slowly the light came back into his eyes, and he looked up at me. I knew now, after dealing with the smaller seizures he'd been having, that he was going to be okay.

"I'm sorry, Mark," he rasped, "so sorry. Did I break anything? Let me get up and—"

"Shh. No, it's okay, babe," I told him and rubbed his chest. "Nothing got broken. And you're going to stay there 'til you feel a hundred percent. Now tell me, are you okay? Does anything hurt?"

He sighed and relaxed back down on the sofa. "How bad was it?"

"Not bad at all, sweetheart. I wasn't paying attention, so forgive me? I just wasn't watching," I apologized.

"Now you hush," he chuckled. "Not a damn thing for you to say you're sorry for. This isn't your fault."

"I know. But it hurts to see this happen to you. I want to take it away and fix it and make it all better for you. I just can't…." I said as my voice broke. He pulled me down on his chest, and I started to silently cry right on top of him. I reached my arms around him and pulled him in close and just hugged until I got control of my emotions again.

He comforted me when it should have been me being strong for him.

"Let's go back and try to eat something. I think I can keep it down and your lasagna is just too good to waste, babe," he joked. He was able to stand under his own power and made it back to the table. I went to the kitchen and got him a clean fork and we sat down to finish our meal, all thoughts of Antonio left behind.

Monday I was calling the doctor and demanding some more tests. I had to know what was wrong with him.

CHAPTER NINE

January 2004

I WAS on my way to take my last box of personal items out to my car when Dan called out to me. "Mark, are you about done? Anything you need some help with?"

"No, this is the last load, then I'll be headed out. Has everybody else already gone? Am I the cow's tail?" I joked.

I went in and sat down, taking in the emptiness of the office. Dan'd already taken all of his things out too, it looked like. "I think you and I are it. Isn't it always the finance and money guys who bring up the rear? But yes, it's just us two then we can turn out the lights," he said. He looked around and like me, was reluctant to leave.

"I'm going to miss this place. The work we do. You." This was the first time we had to ourselves since the board of directors voted to close shop after the loss of our major city grant. All of the good wishes and warm fuzzy promises don't mean shit when the money goes kaput. And fuck the bastards on the city council sideways. Self-serving, arrogant pricks.

"I know you don't like praise much, but it's been an honor working with you these past six years," I told him, knowing this was my last opportunity. "I've learned so much, and I know I can be a bear to work with, but you always just listened and were fair to me. And never made me feel like I was wrong. I'll take that with me to Hope House."

He looked at me with that slight smile that barely drew up the corners. Fuck, the first month I worked here I thought Dan was British;

he was so tight-assed and… frigid. Then I slowly got to know him and realized he was just a dry version of me. Same smart-ass attitude, but mine was loud and in-your-face while his was quiet and needle-sharp.

I considered him one of my best friends, and I would miss working with him more than I ever thought.

"Mark, the pleasure's been all mine. We made a difference here. We had some good times. And we didn't do anything but the best we could. Right?"

Damn. He knew, as he always did, what I was really thinking. I felt, deep down, that there was something more we could've done, someone we didn't talk to, a funder we didn't reach out to.

"Right?" he asked again, raising one eyebrow.

"Right." I smiled at him. And almost, *almost* believed it. And probably, someday, I would. But not today.

"Then let's take this last box out for you, lock the door, and get the fuck out of here and have a drink," he said.

I HAD the week off before I started my new job. I was honestly torn between being excited and scared shitless. The new position I'd found was as the chief financial officer for an agency that worked with kids in foster care. It was my first time being totally responsible for the whole financial running of an agency, but I knew I was good at what I did.

And this cause was so fucking important that I wanted to get it right. After seeing the way Brian was still hurting after his experiences in the foster care system, I knew I could make a difference.

"Are you looking forward to starting your new job next week?" Brian asked.

We were lying in bed, just relaxing and listening to John Mayer and talking. It'd been a long day for him, work and then a doctor's appointment, another test with no clear result, and then we went out to eat. That way we could kick back when we got home. The more tired he was, the worse the slight shaking that was in his hands sometimes got.

"Yeah, I am. I think I can do good work for Hope House. Those kids'll have everything I can give them and more. But what I want to talk about is you. How're you feeling tonight, babe?"

I rolled over and straddled him, looking down at him. God, he was so beautiful. To look, you would never know—no, I wouldn't think about that. Not tonight. I reached down and brushed my lips across his, not quite kissing yet but letting him know what was coming. Soon.

"I feel good, Mark. Just was a little tired from the day. You know all that doctor stuff. Hurry up and wait to get in, then sit there for half an hour to be seen. But thanks for taking me out to dinner. We haven't done that in a while," he said while chasing my kisses.

"Mmmm, well, you just lay back and let me take care of things for you then," I whispered into his mouth, then slowly touched my lips to his. After the day he had, I wanted to make him feel good. Make it better for him. Show him he was loved still. That nothing was changed. Fix things. Him.

My tongue slid across his bottom lip, then pushed its way in. I ran it over his front teeth, then around in a lazy circle. It touched his tongue and I took the kiss deeper, closing my mouth more firmly to his. I could feel his moan more than hear it, and I sucked at his tongue, feeling his cock start to harden in his sleep pants.

I leaned back a little so I could look at his face and take in what I saw there. "I love you, Brian," I said. I saw the happiness, the love, the passion and excitement, and the sadness there, swirling around and dancing in the bright blues and silvers of his beautiful eyes.

"Love you too, Mark. So much, so very much," he moaned.

I moved my mouth back to his and placed slow kisses on his mouth, then moved to suck on his earlobe. The whole time I straddled his body, but I kept the contact to a minimum. This was for him, all about him, and I wanted his body lit up and alive.

My mouth found its way down his jaw and to his throat. I could feel his pulse in his neck, the excitement right under his skin, moving all through his veins. I sucked against his collarbone for a minute, then allowed my mouth to move down his body.

"Please," he whispered. "Please."

I wanted this to last and didn't answer. I moved to the other side and licked a long trail across his neck and paused to kiss and lightly nibble. I put my mouth right over his left nipple and puffed warm hot air onto it. The skin began to tighten and pebble up, and I licked it with just the tip of my tongue, pulled on the ring with my tongue.

Something like a sob came out of his mouth, but he kept his hands bunched in the sheets and closed his eyes. God, what he did to me. I lowered my mouth over it and bit the tiny tip slightly, worried it between my teeth just like he liked. I tugged the piercing with my teeth 'til the moans broke out of his throat and his breath got more shallow and raspy. Then I moved across to the other one and gave it the same treatment.

"Oh, God, I want you to stop, don't stop, bite it, please just bite me," he breathed. I don't even know if he knew what he was asking for at this point.

Now that I had him where I wanted him, I moved my mouth lower still, licking between his pecs and down to his stomach, slowly… slowly… slowly. I trailed across his abs. They were nice and smooth, not ripped but tight and powerful. I darted my tongue into his navel and teased him there, sucking and licking.

I shifted backward and sat up, finally touching him with my hands, and nudged him on both sides of his hips so he would lift them and let me slide his sleep pants down. I rolled to the side slightly and pulled them off.

His cock flopped up against his belly and lay there, pulsing with his heartbeat. His balls were full and hanging, like two ripe figs. I straddled his legs and sucked one in, rolling it on my tongue, then tugging it away from his body with my teeth.

The sounds he was making were incredible. Moans, gasps, sobs. He loved it when I used my mouth on him, and I was going to show him how much I loved and needed him.

I moved my attention to his other ball, not touching it with my hands, just my mouth. And he knew, knew not to move and not to touch. Tonight I would've allowed it, but no words needed to be spoken. His gasps and moans told me what I needed to know.

I let his balls slip out and turned my head slightly sideways so I could suck the base of his cock. I grabbed it between my teeth lightly and moved up and down the shaft, almost up to the head, but stopped short with every stroke. I ran my tongue up and down the vein. My warm breath made the movement gentle and almost frictionless.

When I saw his thighs tremble with the want and need he felt for me, I took pity on him and edged forward and sucked the head into my mouth, making his cock stand upright. I started slowly, running my tongue in circles on the glans while I took in a couple of inches at a time.

I finally reached down and held his hips in place. But not before I grabbed his hands and moved them to my head to let him know, yes, it was okay to take his pleasure. Wordlessly, I gave him the control.

When his hands were locked in my short, straight hair, I took in all of his cock. Deep into my throat. I didn't suck cock often, but I knew what I was doing and how to make it feel good. I slid my hands under his hips and grabbed two handfuls of that ass, that gorgeous ass I loved so much. And I sucked. I sucked him deep and drew his ass up and fucked my face with his body.

He got the point and began to pump his hips forward. He held my head in place with his hands and got depth and sweet friction. The pace was slow at first, because I wanted it to last and to be so good for him. And it was, I could tell. I lost myself in the rhythm.

I could feel the tension and the increase in speed. He was getting close. My tongue worked the sweet nerve bundle right under the slit, above where the knot of his circumcision scar was. His breath was fast, almost panting, and his hands flexed in my hair, gripping and pulling.

I slid my hands further under his ass and spread his cheeks and let my index fingers brush close to his hole, and he lost it. I heard him grunt and cry out, and then his cock grew thick and hard and the waves of his load started to splash in my mouth and throat.

I swallowed down every drop and kept the suction on his cock hard and steady until he gave a big shiver and his hips dropped back onto the bed. His breath came in big gulps and his hands released my hair. I let his cock slide out of my mouth and licked up and down the shaft, and made sure he was cleaned.

I moved up over him and put my mouth right against his again and let his breath whoosh out into my mouth. I slowly captured his lips in a kiss, light and gentle. He relaxed into it and reached up again to hold me by the back of the neck and deepened the kiss, but never took it over. He met me man to man, and I let him.

When he began to cry, I kept kissing him. Wordlessly filled him with my heart and love until the quiet shower of his pain and grief spent itself. I held him until he slept, stroked his hair and cradled him in my arms.

MY OFFICE at Hope House was fan-freaking-tastic. It was huge, and I had enough seating room for a table and three chairs so I could have meetings. This CFO gig was the *shit*!

The executive team had a meet and greet with all the managers, and I could tell I made the right decision to work here. The kids in our care were teens, victims of abuse, physical, sexual, mental, all had histories that most people can't imagine. And Hope House provided counseling and housing for them, twenty-four hours every day, all year long. The kids came from all over the state of Georgia, all in foster care, taken from their homes and in need of care. These kids were special, though. They needed a little more counseling and a more structured setting than a regular foster family could provide, so they were referred to places like Hope House to live.

On my first day there, I got to go back to the cafeteria and have lunch with the kids. Or, as we called them, residents. Because this was their home, at least for now. We tried hard to make them feel it was a safe place for them to heal.

At any given time there were about forty residents, half boys and half girls. Since I handled all the finances, it included any money the residents had on account and funds for their weekend outings. Before I'd even been settled in for four hours, they already knew who I was.

And so the campaigning began. The group of five boys I sat with looked me over and exchanged glances. I watched out of the corner of my eye, and this young guy who looked to be about thirteen or fourteen jumped in with both feet.

"So they tell me you're the man to talk to about getting us some money to go to the movies this weekend," he said.

This wasn't my first time at the rodeo. I don't have a passel of nieces and nephews and not learn a few tricks of the trade. "Who are *they*? And you are…?" I asked.

"The staff. They said we have a new money man, and you're who we're supposed to ask about our money," the young man explained. "And I'm Robbie. What's your name?"

"*They* didn't tell you? Your information isn't too good then, is it, Robbie?" I shot back. He looked at me for a minute and I wasn't sure which way this was going to go. When I met with the clinical director, she told me to treat all the kids just like I would any other teenager, because that's what they were, teenagers who needed to be treated normally. But this interaction would probably set the tone for how they looked at me. This group anyway. And they would talk.

"Mr. Mark. And today's your first day. When can we talk about money for that movie this weekend?" He grinned. "And we want popcorn too. And Cokes. Candy would be good too, but you can't see a movie without popcorn and a Coke, can you, Mr. Mark? Isn't there a law or something?" the little shit asked.

I couldn't help it. I burst out laughing and that made them all laugh. "I tell you what, Robbie, how about I talk to your staff and we can see what's up for the weekend? If they say you guys are good to go, then I'll see what I can do to make that happen. Good deal?"

"Good deal, man," he said and stuck his hand out. I reached out to take it and he jerked it back, then laughed. Then stuck it back out and grabbed my hand and did one of those convoluted handshake things I never was any damn good at.

I knew then that everything was going to be just fine.

CHAPTER TEN

May 2004

ANTONIO was in a bit of a strange mood when I got over to his apartment that evening. It was his birthday, and I knew turning thirty could be really weird for some guys, but he was always unconcerned about age. I really didn't think that was what was going on.

I took him out to dinner and things were fine. We went to The Colonnade because, well, it made me laugh to see all the queens drool over him, and the blue-haired ladies clutch their purses and pearls. He had that whole Vin Diesel vibe going that made the bottom boys quiver. And the tattoos and the attitude just screamed James Dean in *Rebel Without a Cause* to the older crowd.

Of course, he was fucking clueless about both. The hot, steamy looks went right over his head, and the fear, well, he just didn't care. So we had a couple of drinks with dinner, then went to the movies. *Van Helsing* was out and I got my eye candy with Hugh Jackman and he got to see Kate Beckinsale and we both left the theater happy men.

When we got back to his apartment was when things went a little wonky. I gave him his present—D&G cologne and bath gel, 'cause damn, but that stuff smelled like sex on him—and he liked it. So did I. We had a couple of glasses of wine and were good and relaxed. And then his mood just went... off a couple of bubbles left of center.

Did I call out the elephant in the room, or let him get around to it? As laid back as I was, and it being his birthday and all, I figured the best bet was to let him tell me when he was ready. Seemed like we did this dance a lot lately. He got all quiet and looked at me funny.

It was our regular Thursday night together, so I decided to ask him if he wanted his massage first. Over the years, this kind of was a back and forth thing. Sometimes he went first, sometimes I did. It was nice, and not every week ended up with a massage, but that was okay too. "How about since you're the birthday boy, I give you your massage first?" I asked.

"Hmmm? Okay, that sounds fine," he said. But I could tell he wasn't really paying close attention. Something really was on his mind. I knew how to set up the table, so while he went to take a piss, I got things together and even heated up the oil. I lit a couple of candles and put on my favorite music. He went first, I picked the music. My rules. So I put on Loreena McKennitt and really got into the mood.

He came out of the bedroom already stripped down and looked at the table. He seemed surprised I already had everything all set up, but climbed on facedown and settled in. I stripped down then and rubbed the oil into my hands then started on his back. The muscles were tense, but I kneaded and stroked until I could almost feel his sigh when he let go and relaxed. I kept up the steady, deep pressure and finally got him to the point where his muscles were loose and his arms hung over the side of the table.

I had him turn over and started on his chest. His tension level dropped down to almost nothing. Thank God. Maybe he'd talk about it. I just couldn't figure out where his mood swings came from sometimes. It wasn't money, because I knew that business had been good. In fact, Antonio was picking up work doing custom laptop installations and setting up software. He kind of just taught himself to do all that kind of hardware and software stuff while waiting for business. He spent most mornings and early afternoons on the computer chatting up potential clients.

When I was done with him, we swapped off, and I took my place on the table. He had such damn good hands that the stress just melted out of my muscles. I was almost dozing by the time he finished with my back and legs, and when he tapped my foot to tell me to turn over— stick a fork in me, I was done.

But I flipped over and settled down again and he started with my chest. It was almost always the same routine: chest, arms, hips, legs, back up the other side and ending up behind my head while he massaged my temples and scalp. I swear I could almost feel myself purring like a cat.

This time, though, something different happened. I felt his hands still on the sides of my head. I opened my eyes and looked up to see if something was wrong. He looked down at me with something that looked like a cross between sadness and hope.

Then he bent down and gently kissed me.

I WAS too shocked to say anything right then. The kiss was so light I could almost say it didn't happen. But it did. His lips were against mine, then he pulled back and looked back down at me. His eyes were so open, so clear, and all I could do was hold my breath.

Then he bent down and kissed me again. I felt his tongue as it pressed against my lips and for a minute, I forgot myself and kissed him back. But then I remembered who I was and who he was, and he must have felt the tension in me. Because he pressed his lips to mine one more time then drew back.

"Antonio," I started, my voice low and raspy at first. "What—" He brought a finger up and put it over my lips to make me be quiet.

"Shh. It's okay. I just wanted to see. It's okay. I know you have Brian, but I just had to know...." He looked confused and sad.

"Know what?" I asked, shaking off the finger on my lips.

"Know what it felt like. Know what *you* felt like," he said, resignation in his voice.

"And?" I was curious but almost afraid to hear the answer.

He shrugged and I saw his eyes close and his face shut down. He started to move away but I wasn't going to let something like that pass without knowing what the fuck was going on in his head. My very straight best friend kissed me? Oh *hell* no.

I jumped up off the table and grabbed his wrist to stop him. I pulled him around and stood there face-to-face with him and didn't let him go.

"I asked you how it felt. But Antonio, what were you thinking? What were you doing?" I demanded.

He stood there and looked me eye to eye. I had to give him credit for that, because had the situations been switched, I think I would've hauled ass for the hills. It wasn't that I was mad, just surprised. I was attracted to him and had known that for years. So did he. But I would never have cheated on Brian, first of all. And second, Antonio was *straight.*

"I wanted to see what the big deal was. You're my best friend and I love you. And I know you're with Brian, but I just had to know what it was like to kiss you. To be with you that way. It didn't mean anything. Please, Mark, don't let it mean anything bad. I just wanted to know," he whispered.

"Antonio, I'm not mad. Dude, I love you too. But you aren't into guys. I mean, you haven't ever been with one before, have you? You said no, before, but have you?" I asked.

"No, I haven't ever had sex with a dude. Well, other than...." He blushed. "Never even kissed one for real until tonight. Shit, Mark, I never even wanted to before really other than you." His eyes begged me to believe him and to let it go.

Not going to happen.

"So do you think you might be bi now? Is it because of doing the massages? Seeing all those guys naked and you just got curious? And maybe I'm just safe because you know me? Help me out some here, man." I really wanted to understand.

"No, man. I see guys naked all the time and never wanted to do anything with them. And really, man, fuck, you ain't the safe one. You're my best friend and I don't want to fuck up anything. I know I'm not the best friend in the world, and you already had to bail my ass out once, so, man, please. Tell me I didn't fuck anything up," he pleaded.

"Of course you didn't. Antonio, it was only a little kiss. It didn't mean anything. I'm okay, and you're okay. So don't worry about it. Got it?" I told him.

He looked at me, searched in my eyes to really make sure it was all good. Whatever he saw there seemed to reassure him, and his shoulders dropped and the tension left his body. I looked down and saw I was still holding his wrist hard, where I'd grabbed him to keep him there.

"Okay, Mark, okay," he breathed. I pulled him against me into a hug, and felt the tension grip him again. But I didn't let go and, after a minute, he hugged me back. A full-blown, full-body hug that told me in that moment more than what his mouth had danced around.

He cared about me, probably more than he should, and I didn't know what to do with it. But he was my best friend, and I damn well *would* figure it out. He was as damn confused about this as I was. We got dressed and met back in the den.

We had another glass of wine and sat there on his couch, mostly in silence. But it was a comfortable silence, and that was fine. There wasn't a lot to say right then, and I had to work the next day so I got all my stuff together and got ready to leave.

"Happy birthday, old man, and many, many more," I said.

"Thanks. It's been a great one and I appreciate you taking me out. I have Jason this weekend and he's got something he made for me, so I don't know what to expect." He laughed.

"I'm sure whatever it is, you'll love it. Call me if you two decide to go to a movie or something. Brian and I're having dinner with my dad on Saturday night, but Sunday is mostly free."

"Will do. Drive safe." He always told me that before I left. He walked behind me to the door, and before I reached out to open it, I turned around. I looked him directly in the eye and pulled him into a hug and kissed him. On the cheek.

"Sweet dreams," I murmured into his ear, then went out and closed the door behind me.

WHEN I got home, Brian was propped up in the bed reading a magazine. He loved reading about sports cars and mechanical shit like that. I knew how to put gas in a car, and could usually find the dipstick to check the oil in an emergency. But that was what was good about us; we both had different interests and didn't mind that the other wasn't so much into them.

"How was your night?" he asked, patting the bed beside him.

I pulled off my clothes and put on a pair of sleep pants. I could never manage to sleep in the nude. In the back of my mind, I was always afraid the house would catch on fire and I'd be running around outside bare-assed. I'd actually had a dream like that one time when I was a teenager, and it still scared the crap out of me.

"It was pretty good. I took Antonio out to The Colonnade, then to see that new Hugh Jackman movie. We sat and talked for a while afterwards. Got a good massage and then home to you," I told him. "How was your night?"

"Not bad. I took a nap, watched some TV, and talked to your sister on the phone. They're all good, just checking in. She said to call her this weekend."

I crawled into bed and bunched my pillows up against the headboard next to him. I rested my head on his shoulder and sighed. It was good to be home and in the bed. I could relax and think over what happened earlier.

"You going to tell me what's on your mind, or do we have to play twenty questions?" he asked. I never knew how he knew when something was bothering me, because I know I didn't show it. "You always sigh and all that shit when you have something you're thinking hard about. You know I'll listen and help if I can."

I breathed out a sigh and caught myself. Shit, I *did* do that. "That's just creepy that you can do that. Something happened tonight and I don't know what to make of it."

"Um hum. And what was that something?" he asked and put his magazine down. He pulled my head down from his shoulder and into his lap. "Mmmm, you got a massage again. I love the smell of that almond oil he uses. So good. Makes me think of cookies." He laughed.

"Antonio kissed me," I blurted. Jesus, where did that come from? I'd planned to ease into this conversation, and here I practically shouted it at him.

"Is that all?" he asked while he stroked my hair.

I was fucking stunned and didn't know what the hell to say now. "What do you mean, *Is that all?*" I choked out. "Isn't that enough?"

"Okay, I'll play along here. Did you ask him to?" he sighed.

"No, of course not," I huffed.

"Did you kiss him back?" That one stopped me. Because I didn't. At first. But then I kinda sorta did. "And was that all that happened?" he asked. Shit, I'd said all of that out loud.

"Of course it is! I'd never cheat on you, you know that." I did shout that time.

"Hush. I know you wouldn't. I'm the one who did that. And you forgave me. Best day of my life," he said as he leaned over and kissed my ear.

"Brian, that's not what I meant—"

"Shh. I know that. But nothing bad happened, did it? All you did was give each other massages and then come home, right?"

I jerked my head up, and he fucking *laughed* at me. "Mark, you only get that much oil on your hands by massaging somebody or jacking off. And I know you weren't using it to jack off." He snorted. "I trust you. You would've told me if anything was going on. I know you."

My heart was just so full of love for this fucking man. How did I ever think I would live without him? How could I? I laid my head back in his lap and thought for a minute. Then I told him what happened. All of it. Including when I hugged and kissed him on the cheek before I left.

"He loves you," Brian said.

"Well, yeah, I love him too. He's my best friend. After you," I told him.

"No, Mark. He *loves* you. He's in love with you." He looked at me with amusement and pity.

"No fucking way. He's straight. This was just an experiment. Trust me, he'll be back to talking about pussy and girl toes and all that shit tomorrow and everything'll be back to normal," I said. I was certain of it. Antonio wasn't in love with me. He was straight. He had a son. He slept with women.

And I was with Brian and that wasn't going to change. So no, he wasn't in love with me. Brian just stroked my hair and we both lay there.

CHAPTER ELEVEN

ABOUT two weeks later, I'd committed to go on an outing with a group of the kids at work. Because the weather was nice, some of the staff members were taking a picnic lunch to Piedmont Park, and I'd volunteered to come and bring my dogs. Since it was a weekend, Brian was coming with me. He really liked to help with the kids when there was an opportunity.

I'd also invited Antonio and Jason. In all the time I'd known Antonio, this was the first time the three, or really four, of us had spent any time together. Ever. Brian and I bundled the two dogs up and put their pink and purple collars on them. They also had matching bandanas, but they were gay enough with the collars and rainbow leashes. Their names were Lucy and Ricky.

Antonio and Jason were meeting us there, and I was looking forward to the day. But I was a little nervous too. Brian loved kids and I knew he and Jason would be fast friends. Anybody Jason liked, Antonio liked. It was just I really, really wanted them all to be friends.

Robbie was one of the residents that would be at the park. Since I met him my first day on the job, he'd decided I was cool enough to talk to. So I made it a point to try to sit and eat lunch with him whenever I made it to the cafeteria. He was forever trying to get me to commit to more outings and more money for them to do things on the weekends.

I'd looked at his admission file and never would've known his history from the times I was around him. Both parents were in prison for child abuse and neglect, as well as drug trafficking. He and his sister were committed to foster care, but his sister was taken in by an aunt. There was no room for him at the aunt's home, and she was quite vocal, evidently, in telling him he wasn't wanted. So unless he was adopted or taken into a private foster family, he'd stay in a group home until he turned eighteen and aged out of the system.

There was a notation of drug abuse and prostitution in his history. And he was only fourteen now. Prostitution. That broke my heart. This beautiful and funny and alive kid, and he'd suffered all of that in his short life. He got the treatment he needed and deserved now, though.

The staff arrived with the kids shortly after Brian and I got to the park. We set up with blankets on the ground and tossed a Frisbee and let the dogs chase us around some to take the edge off their energy. They were miniature pinschers and thought they ruled the world. And well, they did pretty much.

When Robbie spotted us and caught sight of the dogs, his eyes lit up like it was Christmas. He ran over and flopped down on the ground and the two little beasts attacked him. It was love at first sight. I looked over at Brian and saw the look on his face and my heart melted all over that fucking meadow. Brian would've made such a terrific dad, or even older brother.

I hadn't really shared anything with any of the staff or kids about my sexual orientation, but I did keep pictures of Brian and me on my desk. Everyone was welcome there, and I always believed in an open door policy. I also kept a big bowl of candy on the table in my office to welcome anyone who wanted to come in. And I was pretty popular with staff and kids because of that.

But this was the first time Brian and I'd been *together* together at a work-related function. He volunteered one-on-one, yeah, but that was as an individual. I wasn't going to fuck him there, and I really wasn't a fan of PDAs, but I do like to be who I am around other people. In my interview, that obviously wasn't something they could ask, but I brought it up. I certainly couldn't work for an agency that wasn't inclusive or at a minimum tolerant.

As it turned out, the executive director was also gay. His belief was that some of the kids Hope House served were gay and deserved appropriate adult role models of all shapes, sizes, and flavors. It took a village to raise a child, and it took a rainbow of colors to make them feel at home and comfortable.

Robbie rolled around on the grass with Lucy and Ricky, and before long Brian was right there with him. Some of the other kids came over to watch, but none of them joined in right then. They were busy eyeing the Frisbee and the food the staff were setting up.

"Mr. Mark, are these your dogs? I love them. They're like shrunk-down little Dobermans. Are they babies or will they get any bigger?" Robbie asked.

"These're miniature pinschers. This is Lucy," I pointed to my girl in the pink collar, "and Ricky. They're fully grown. We got them three years ago, so they won't get any bigger."

Robbie looked at me, then at the dogs, then at Brian. "You're the guy in the pictures in Mr. Mark's office," he said as he squinted at us.

"Robbie, this is Brian," I said. He looked at me for a very long moment, then looked over at Brian and made the connection.

"Mr. Mark's a nice guy. He makes sure we have money to do fun things. And he has lunch with me in the cafeteria. I'm glad you came with him today," he said.

"Robbie, it's really good to meet you," Brian said and stuck out his hand. The three of us chatted for a few minutes, but Lucy and Ricky had other ideas. They nipped and barked at Robbie, sensing an easy mark. He jumped up and started to tease the dogs and took off running in circles with them. God, I hoped he ran their energy out of them and they slept like babies later. Those two loved nothing more than to play and run with kids. They would jump and push my nephews and nieces down and stand on top of them to claim their alpha-hood. Damn beasts.

"He seems like a great kid," Brian said.

"You have no idea how great. He's the one I told you about, no family contact and the abuse and stuff. The therapy is doing him good, but he's still struggling with fitting in. He misses his sister a lot, and for some reason, he just doesn't seem to be making a lot of friends," I told him.

"Well, he certainly is a fan of yours," he laughed.

"Yeah," I said, as I watched him play with the dogs. God, he really was such a good kid. Any family would be lucky as hell to have him in their lives. I wasn't stupid, and I knew the challenges he had. He had been pimped out and hooked on drugs, and that made some kids hard and angry. Where some kids sexualized at a young age were manipulative and adultlike, Robbie somehow became socially awkward and younger than his physical age. He didn't show it often, but he had a tendency to have an explosive temper when he was pushed too hard. He also could lapse into depression when he thought too hard about his life and past. That was why he functioned better at Hope House for now.

But I wanted the best for this boy. Since I started work there, I'd seen kids come and go. Robbie would be there for a long while. And honestly, there was just such a capacity for joy and love that he kept hidden from most people. I was lucky he'd shown it to me.

I looked around and caught sight of Antonio and Jason making their way across the field toward us. I stood up and waved them over, and just like Robbie, when Jason caught sight of the dogs, he ran to jump into the fun. Antonio sauntered over and took a seat on the blanket with us.

"Hey, man, how're you doing today?" he asked and looked over at Brian, a question on his face.

"Good, how're you? Antonio, this is Brian. Brian, Antonio," I said and made the introductions. "And that ball of energy is Jason."

"It's really good to finally meet you, Antonio. Mark's told me all about you guys and what a good friend you are. And he really loves Jason too," Brian said and nodded toward the boy. Antonio looked at him, then me, and weighed what he saw.

Then he grinned and held his hand out. "It's real good to meet you too, Brian. Mark talks about you all the time, man, and I've been wanting to meet you forever."

"Same here. I think Mark's been hiding you all for himself," he drawled and looked over at me.

"Hey! There's more than enough of me to go around," I joked back.

"You sure about that, baby?" Antonio asked, his eyebrows raised. Brian looked at me and I could see it in his face, that little lift of his lips. *Baby?*

We all laughed. That seemed to loosen things up. We sat and talked and shot the shit while the boys played with the dogs. Robbie and Jason got along famously and soon came over to sit down shoulder to shoulder on the blanket, each holding a dog. Antonio chatted with Brian and watched the two of us with thoughtful eyes. He kept looking at Brian with something in his face, like he was putting puzzle pieces together.

He talked and laughed and played with Jason and the dogs. And he included Brian in the conversation so things were fine. Comfortable. If it hadn't been for the rest of the staff and kids, it would've felt like a family outing. And wasn't that a kick in the seat of the pants. And something to think about later.

LATER in the afternoon, after lunch, everyone sat around relaxed and enjoying the day. The sounds of conversation and laughter drifted across the field. Staff members and kids were spread wide and a good time was had. Robbie was sitting with Brian and me.

Antonio and Jason had left to go back home, but not before we had to practically force Jason to go with his dad. It was good to see the two of them get along so well; Jason could be a little standoffish, and Robbie didn't make friends easily. He and Robbie were having a great time, though, and he didn't want to leave his new friend. They said their good-byes, though, and Antonio stared at Brian again for a moment then left. Brian was on his stomach while he lightly dozed and Robbie sat next to me on the blanket.

"Mr. Mark, can I tell you something? I don't want you to tell anybody. Can I trust you?" he asked. I looked at him. He was so earnest. I knew if it was something important, that I'd have to disclose it to his therapist. But I wouldn't betray his trust. I couldn't.

"Yeah, Robbie, you can trust me," I told him. He waited a minute, and studied his sneakers. When he did speak, it was in a low voice and loaded with emotion.

"I'm gay," he said so very quietly.

"Robbie, look at me," I told him. He looked up at me and his eyes were heavy with tears that I just knew would spill over at any second.

"Robbie, it's okay. Do you hear me? It's okay. It doesn't change anything. Have you told anyone else?" I asked. He would know why I was asking. It could affect his therapy.

"My therapist. She knows. Nobody else. Nobody wants me and now nobody will 'cause nobody wants a faggot for a son," he whispered and tears slid down his cheeks. He didn't even reach up to wipe them away.

Fuck. This boy, this giant-hearted boy didn't deserve to hurt like this. I wasn't supposed to touch him, because protocols and policies said it could be taken as an inappropriate advance. Fuck that. I pulled that gentle boy by my side and shielded him from the view of everyone else and hugged him with one arm. Let his silent sobs flow until they ran their course. I picked up one of towels we had brought for the pups to lay on and wiped his eyes and nose.

"Now you listen to me and you listen good," I told him. "You're a wonderful, beautiful boy, and any family would be stupid to not want you. You are *not* a faggot, and never let me hear you use that word again. That's a filthy word, and you're too good to use that kind of language. Don't you ever think that you are anything but a good boy, you hear me?"

I felt his nod against my side. "Mr. Mark?" his whisper drifted up to my ears.

"Yeah, Robbie?" I said.

"I wish I was yours. I wish I was your son and I could come live with you and Mr. Brian, and have dogs like Lucy and Ricky. I'd try to make you really proud," he breathed.

God damn it. My fucking heart broke and my own tears spilled down. I choked down a sob before I could answer him. This was not the place to be having this kind of conversation. I wondered what was going on with Robbie that his emotions were running this close to the surface. He was usually a lighthearted kid, making jokes and avoiding serious feelings and discussions. In fact, the discussions I had heard were around how he wasn't making progress dealing with his therapeutic goals. Then I remembered. He wanted to see his sister and his aunt had said no. His therapist was trying to arrange a family session and not meeting with any cooperation.

"Me too, Robbie. And if it was possible, I would. I *would*. You just remember, your sister loves you. It isn't her that's saying no right now. You stay brave, okay?" I said. And I meant it. That boy had wormed his way into my heart and I loved him. Wanted the best for him. Right at that moment, I hated his parents, hated his aunt.

I looked over at Brian and saw his open eyes, so wide open, like his heart. And so full of love and pain, just like mine. And I saw him mouth to me, "I love you so much."

That's all it took. I let all the hate go and just sat there, one arm around Robbie, listening to the quiet sounds of the fun winding down. We all sat there deep in our thoughts until the afternoon drifted into evening and we all had to go back to our homes.

CHAPTER TWELVE

December 2004

WHEN I got in to the office that Monday after Christmas, I knew something was wrong immediately. I'd taken the week off and felt relaxed and ready to get back to work. Usually the kids were at breakfast and I would see staff taking various boys or girls back and forth between buildings, and there was an air of activity. I didn't hear any background noise, and Lisa Franklin, one of the therapists, was waiting outside my office.

Not a good sign.

I greeted her and opened up my door and asked her to come in. I took a deep breath and turned to face her. "Lisa, what's wrong? This place feels... hollow or something." She sat on the edge of my desk and just looked at me for a moment. Finally, she sighed.

"A group of boys ran last night. Six of them," she started. "They waited 'til shift change and kicked the door open. Four of them came back. The police picked up one and he's in detention."

I knew. I dreaded what she was going to say next but I already knew.

"Robbie. He ran, didn't he? He's the one that isn't back," I stated flatly. No question there. She nodded. And I felt cold and numb and didn't know I'd missed something 'til Lisa kept repeating my name. I looked up and blinked.

"Mark, he left you a note," she gently said.

No. I couldn't. I didn't want to know.

I hadn't realized I was speaking out loud. "Don't blame yourself. This was a choice Robbie made, Mark. He was placed here for reason," she said.

Oh, fuck you too. I knew why he did it. He'd wanted to come to my house on Christmas Morning and it was against policy, and I was told, in no uncertain terms, that it wasn't a fight I was going to win. I mean, I understood the reasons. Other kids got jealous. Kids formed inappropriate attachments to staff. Staff leave. Kids leave.

My heart left.

She handed me the piece of notebook paper, folded over with "Mr. Mark" written on it. "Want me to stay?" she asked gently. I shook my head. She left and quietly shut the door behind her.

I looked at the note, and then after I grabbed my balls in one hand and my courage in the other, I opened it and read.

Dear Mr. Mark,

I have to go. They won't let me see my sister and you can't take me home with you. Nobody wants me. I hate being here. Christmas sux. I know somebody that will let me stay with him and it won't be bad. I knew him before.

Before I go I want to tell you I love you. Thank you for being my friend. Please tell Lucy and Ricky I will miss them and to be good and maybe you and Mr. Brian can take them to the park one day and they will be happy and have fun.

It's better this way. Another kid who needs to be here can have my bed.

I will miss you. This is better though. He don't care that I am gay. And I can work for him and maybe one day I can make enough money to have a minature pincher for me and an apartment.

Love, your friend,

Robbie Gordon

Why was it raining inside my office, I thought. There were drops of rain on the letter.

HOW long I sat there I couldn't tell you. Eventually I picked up the phone and called Brian and let him know what'd happened. "Come home, sweetheart. Take the rest of the day off and come on home," he said.

"I'll be okay. I think if I work, I won't worry so much about it. And maybe he'll come back. Maybe they'll find him," I said, more to convince myself than him.

"If he doesn't want to be found, he won't be. He's a smart kid. Let him cool off and he might come back. He said he knew somebody. Is there any note in his file who he... who... the man who he knew when he was tricking," he said gently.

"Oh fuck, Brian, he can't. He wouldn't. I have to talk to Lisa. I'll talk to you later. I love you. Thank you, I didn't even think about that." I hung up and jumped up to go see Lisa again.

I found her in her office. I went in and shut the door. "Lisa," I started before she could say anything, "could he have gone back to Zev? The bastard that was giving him drugs and pimping him out?"

"Why would you think that, Mark?" she asked.

"You read the note. He said he knew someone. And he wants to make money. Can we call the cops?" I wanted to know. She thought about it. Then she reached for the phone and made the call.

She managed to get the officer that took the case information. From the set of her shoulders, I could tell the news wasn't good. "Unfortunately, he can't do much. They'll do a drive-by and take a look to see if he might be there. No promises. And you know the drill. Not a high-priority case," she sadly said.

I just stared. How could a kid on the streets not be a priority? Oh, yeah. There were hundreds on the streets in this fucking city. Well, that didn't mean that I couldn't look for him, I told myself. I wouldn't forget.

A WEEK later I was at Antonio's place, exhausted. After work, I'd been driving all over the Woodruff Park area looking for Robbie. Then I got up at five and patrolled the area and tried to talk to anybody there. No luck and my hope had faded.

Antonio'd opened a bottle of wine and two glasses had kicked my ass. When he got me on the massage table, he started to cuss. "Damn it, Mark. What the fuck?" he asked, concern and anger in his voice. "You're a wreck. Your fucking muscles're jumping. When did you eat something last? Hurting yourself won't help Robbie."

His hands tore into my back, and through sheer force of will he tamed the tension there. I felt myself relax some and before I knew it I started to doze. When he tapped my foot for me to turn over, I almost didn't have the energy to do it. "That's it. Where's your cell phone? I'm calling Brian," he said.

I only heard part of the conversation. The table was padded and I thought, *I could just take a quick nap.* Then I could drive down to Edgewood and see if Robbie was out there tonight.

"Come on, big guy. I talked to your man and you're spending the night here tonight. He'll call your boss in the morning and you can take a sick day. They'll understand," he said.

That got through. "No, man. I have to go check and see if he's out tonight and go home and make sure Brian's okay and that he took his medicine and go to work and check on Robbie in the morning and…."

He pulled me up off the table and put his arm around me. "Shh. It's already decided, baby. Brian said to tell you he loves you and not to worry, he took his meds. When you wake up you're gonna tell me what he needs medicine for. But right now me and him agree on one thing. Your ass is mine tonight," he joked and slapped my bare butt with his big hand.

"In your fucking dreams, straight boy," I managed to joke. He had me in his bedroom now, turned the covers back, and put me under them.

"Sweet dreams, sweet man," he whispered and I felt a brush of lips on my forehead. Then sleep took me.

WHEN I woke up, something was different but I was too groggy to figure out what. I was in bed, on my side, and my guy was behind me with an arm thrown over me and his warm body pressed into me. His morning wood brushed against my thigh. And his breath puffed against my neck.

Nice. I liked being the little spoon sometimes.

So I did what any man would do. I reached back and pulled him closer to me. I really wanted the closeness, needed it. God, the memory of what happened the past week started to creep in and I knew I needed to be held. Two strong arms wrapped around me and pulled me close.

Wait a minute. When did Brian shave down there? And his cock didn't quite feel...

"Morning, baby," Antonio murmured in my ear. I stiffened for a minute, feeling awkward. Then I relaxed and just lay there. God knew I needed someone to touch me. I wanted to lay down my armor, my strength and my pain for just a minute and let someone hold me. I wanted to hide, be protected and not think about Robbie on the streets or Brian's condition.

Please forgive me for being weak, I thought and sent up a silent prayer and plea. I leaned back, closed my eyes, and relaxed into Antonio's strong arms, letting him hold me. He sensed something, my need, my surrender, whatever it was. He went soft and tightened his hold on me, wrapping his arms and legs around me and just surrounded me.

He softly hummed some nameless tune in my ear. I felt myself drifting and I must have dozed off again for a minute. When I woke up again, he slowly loosened his grip on me, rolled over and got up out of bed. "Lay there for a few more minutes. I'm going to put a pot of coffee on and I'll be back in a bit," he said.

He walked out of the bedroom. I rolled over on my back and felt more peace than I had in days. I felt like I'd be able to get through the day now.

Soon enough though, I heard his voice calling out from the kitchen for me to get my ass up and come get a cup. I got up and put on my underwear and jeans and went into the kitchen. I put my hand on his shoulder and brushed my lips against his forehead.

"Thank you," I whispered in his ear.

"Not necessary," he said as he patted my hand.

After I took the coffee from Antonio, and some of my brain cells started to function again, I realized I needed to call Brian. I needed to hear his voice and make sure he was okay. Antonio left the room to give me some privacy.

"Morning, sweetie," his sleepy voice said.

"Hey, sunshine, how're you feeling this morning? Did you take your medicine on time? Any dizziness or—"

"Yes, Mother. I took it last night and this morning already. And no, Mother, I don't have any dizziness or anything else. No seizures. I ate a bagel and laid back down. This bed is empty without you, though, Mother."

"Smart-ass. I should've come home last night. I was okay. But Antonio said he called and you told him you wanted me to stay here. Did you already call work for me?" I asked.

"Damn, I didn't know you wanted to play twenty questions. Yes, he called me and I told him to put you to bed there. He called me back after he made you lay down and said you were out like a light. And snoring. And yeah, I called your boss. Todd said to take the day and get some rest. No new word," he added quietly.

"As long as you're okay. And I don't snore. I think I'll take Antonio out to breakfast to thank him for letting me sleep here last night. Anything you need?" I asked.

"Just for you to come home. And Mark?"

Antonio came back into the room as he pulled on his shirt. "Yeah?" I said, and watched Antonio cover up that broad chest.

"Drive down Edgewood and Auburn Avenue just once. For me," he almost whispered.

My heart broke a little more. This'd hit Brian very hard too. I wondered how many Robbies he'd seen while he was in foster care. How many times he thought about running. How close he came to being on the streets at fourteen, fifteen. I passed a hand over my eyes.

"Yeah, baby, I will. Say a little prayer. Love you and see you later," I said.

"Love you too," he said and hung up. I turned around and started looking for the rest of my clothes. I was grateful. Antonio really did take care of me last night. And this morning. And I felt… cherished.

Once I finished dressing, I saw that Antonio was dressed as well. "Come on, I'm taking you to breakfast. My treat. Thanks for letting me crash here. I didn't know how tired I was," I said.

"No problem. Any time. It was nice to have someone in the bed with me," he said and turned and left the room. He looked embarrassed. I smiled, then it faltered.

It was nice to have someone be strong for me. But I could never say that.

WE HAD breakfast at the Waffle House. I loved their pecan waffles, grits, and hash browns. Looked like I was going to have to get my ass back in the gym. I tried to keep the conversation light. Two things weighed so heavily on my mind, and I had no fucking control over either one. I also really didn't want to get into either with Antonio. I dodged his questions about Brian's meds. Not even my family knew. Well, except Dad. And Mom.

I still went to the cemetery and laid fresh flowers every month. A dozen fresh roses—eleven red and a single white one. Her father, who died before I was born, had told her a story about her grandfather, who was a barber. He had this one client who couldn't pay, and he would always tell the guy, put flowers on my grave when I'm dead. When he died, the guy came to the funeral and put one white rose on the casket. For remembrance. And for years afterward, there would be that one white rose on his grave on the anniversary of his death, and my mom was always so touched by the thought.

So I laid a bouquet once a month, sometimes more if my heart was especially heavy, and talked to her. Now, I knew she wasn't there. In fact, her spirit, soul, whatever was gone two days before her body knew it and gave up. But it gave me comfort to know she listened. Four years later, I still woke up some mornings and felt her love and spirit around me and it was like she had just finished telling me something.

But even my talks with her hadn't eased my heart over the situation with Robbie. I shook myself and brought my attention back to Antonio. He gave me the evil eye and started asking me about Brian's medications and why and what they were for. I wasn't ready for that conversation yet, so I tried to keep the focus on Robbie.

I danced around his questions, which got me more hard looks. I think Antonio saw something in my eyes that let him know I really couldn't talk about Brian right then. With a stare that let me know we were by no means done with this conversation, he sat back and crossed his arms. Thankfully, the waitress chose that moment to come by and drop off the check, so I grabbed it, and we made our way out of the restaurant.

Once we got into the car, I took a deep breath. While I regretted not being able to search the night before, a night of rest and some food had energized me more than I thought. I looked over to Antonio, and before I could even ask, he told me to take a quick drive around the park. "You remember what he looks like, right?" I asked. "He's—"

"Dude, really? I know what he looks like. He spent an afternoon with my kid, I pay attention to the people Jason hangs out with and likes." I could almost see the eye-roll I was sure went along with the smartass comment. "Just be careful driving, and I'll watch out for him. The morning rush is about over, so the crowd should be cleared out. Well, except for the hawkers around Five Points."

I drove as slowly as I could without pissing off the rest of the morning commuters, especially as we got closer to the MARTA station. The homeless and dealers and other folks looking to sell things, both legit and not, hung around this area, and there never seemed to be enough police presence to discourage any of it. Except when some big event came to town, then suddenly the streets were clean and you would walk around downtown without being hit on or hit up.

My gaze roamed the crowds and I hoped. Hoped for just a sight of Robbie to know he was okay. Hoped I could convince him to come back with me. Hoped nothing bad had happened and this hell would all be over. Just… hoped. I was lost in my thoughts when Antonio reached over and grabbed my arm. "There he is, Mark! Pull over, see if you can park somewhere," he nearly shouted. He was as excited as I was.

I saw where he pointed. Robbie was talking to some older guy. I pulled the car over to the edge of the street and jumped out.

"Stay with the car, man. Let me see if I can talk to him," I yelled back to Antonio.

I ran up to where the man was starting to put his hand on Robbie, and he saw me coming and took off, walking fast in the other direction. Robbie turned to me. He looked like he hadn't bathed since he left, and was obviously on something.

"Hey, man, you wanna have a good time? I can suck your—" he started. Then he saw who I was and his face was full of shock. I saw it fall and his eyes tear up. He stood there like frozen to the spot.

"Robbie, let me help. Come with me, please. I promise I'll make it better. I'll fix things. Just come home with me," I begged.

"Home? To your house?" he asked, a glimmer of hope flaring in his eyes through the drugs.

I stuttered for a moment. "No, back to Hope House. I can't take you home, buddy, they won't let you stay with me. I wish I could but I can't. Please," I pleaded. The light in his eyes, that sudden bright light I'd seen, flickered and went dull. He backed away and started running.

"Robbie, come back," I yelled and ran after him. But he had a head start and ducked in and out of the crowd in front of the Five Points MARTA station. I lost sight of him but kept yelling his name. *God, please let me find this boy,* I prayed.

But I couldn't, and after I made another circuit of the area, I finally gave up and went back to the car. "What happened? Where's Robbie?" Antonio asked. He sat in the driver's seat. I climbed in the passenger seat and laid my head back against the headrest and put on my seatbelt.

"Let's just go. He wanted to come back to my house. I fucked up. I told him he couldn't, and he ran again. I fucked up," I said and my voice broke. The fucking tears started again. Antonio reached over and laid a strong hand on my thigh and squeezed.

"Look at me," he said. I couldn't. My eyes were squeezed shut and leaked tears. "Mark, look at me," his voice commanded. I opened my eyes and turned my head on the headrest.

"I'll find him. I'll bring him home to you. I promise you that," he said, voice solid and sure, eyes bright. I was so numb but I wanted to believe him so badly. I nodded and closed my eyes and laid my head back again.

I felt his hand grip my thigh again, and then gentle lips barely touched my cheek.

CHAPTER THIRTEEN

June 2005

THE call came in on my cell phone about an hour after I got into work. "Mr. Jennings?" the voice asked.

"Yes, this is Mark Jennings. May I help you?" I said.

"Mr. Jennings, this is Emily O'Toole at Crawford Long. You're listed as Brian Jacobs's medical contact. Is that correct?" she asked.

"Yes," I said, and all the blood rushed out of my head and I was cold. So cold.

"Mr. Jennings, Mr. Jacobs's been in an accident. I need you to come to the hospital so the doctors can talk to you about his condition. Can you do that for me, Mr. Jennings?" she said, her voice so calm and gentle.

It's June in fucking Atlanta, I thought. Why is it so cold?

"Yes, Ms. O'Toole, I'll be there as soon as I can. Where should I go to?" I managed to get out around the ice.

"Come to the emergency room. Ask for me. I'll coordinate this. How long do you think it'll take you, Mr. Jennings?" that competent voice asked.

"I'm already downtown. I'll be there in fifteen minutes," I said.

"I'll be waiting for you. Please be careful, Mr. Jennings. But please hurry," she said.

Oh God. Hurry. This was it. I'm not ready. Please. I grabbed my keys and a file I kept at hand and, after I ducked in to tell Todd's assistant I had an emergency and would be gone the rest of the day, I got in my car and left.

I MADE it there in thirteen minutes. I parked in front of the emergency room and fucking dared them to tow me. I was inside in another forty-five seconds and demanded to see Emily O'Toole at the nurse's station.

A solid woman with bright red hair came out to meet me. She was a little older than me, maybe forty. A touch over her ideal weight but tall and proud and she had freckles all across her smooth face. I found myself trying to memorize all these small details so I wouldn't have to think about what barreled toward me.

"Mr. Jennings, I'm Emily. I just paged Dr. Amarti, and she'll be here in just a moment. Please come with me," she said. We walked back through the long hallway and stopped in front of a treatment room. The curtain was pulled shut, and I could hear machines and noises inside. I moved to go inside, and she laid a firm but gentle hand on my arm.

God, I hated hospitals. The cool professionalism. How they only saw the illness and the disease and the injuries. Fuck that. They *will* see me. See Brian. They'd done this when my mom died too.

(I stood outside the door, waiting to talk to the internist. Me and my dad. And when he did come, he was all business. I had to make him see me as a person, see Mom as something more than a diagnosis, a note in a chart. Not liver failure. Not another consult. "Call me Mark." Look at me, damn it. "Tell me about my mother." Talk to me. I had to make him see me.)

"Please, Mr. Jennings, would you wait for just a minute. I need to fill you in on what happened before you see Mr. Jacobs. You're aware of his condition?" she asked. I thought I was prepared, I honest to God did, but nothing prepared me for the reality of having this conversation. Not really.

"Please, Emily, call me Mark. *(See me.)* And yes, Brian's my partner. I have his medical power of attorney and living will. I just don't understand, why is he down here? Did they transport him? He was home and Dekalb Medical Center is closer and…."

She looked at me and I saw something cross her face. Understanding. Compassion. Sadness. "I'd really rather wait for Dr. Amarti to get here. She's the attending, and she can tell you options on how we can proceed."

"Just fucking tell me what happened," I said tiredly, all my energy suddenly gone.

"Well, Mark, Brian was evidently driving—"

"What the fuck? He can't drive! His license was taken away after the neurologist made the diagnosis," I practically shouted.

She laid that cool hand back on my arm and I immediately calmed down.

"Please, Mark. I don't know all the details. But from what we've gotten from the paramedics and witnesses, he was driving on Edgewood and had a seizure and lost control of the car. His foot hit the accelerator and he went through two lights and slammed into the side of a building. The airbag deployed, but there was a lot of smoke and a small fire started."

At the mention of fire, my heart skipped a beat and I reached out for her, my knees suddenly jelly under me. That beautiful creature just reached right out and held me up.

("Mr. Jennings. Mark. She probably won't make it through another episode like this again. My recommendation would be that you and your family talk. I know it's a hard call to make, but she indicated she doesn't want to be resuscitated again.")

"Shhh. It's okay, Mark. Fortunately, there were two nurses from here, actually, on their way home after night shift and they saw what happened. They grabbed two or three guys from the construction crew working on the outside of the building and managed to get him out of the car. It took them a little longer than we would've liked it to, but they stabilized him as best they could."

I started to get the strength in my legs back and pulled away from Emily. "Please," I whispered, "please tell me he isn't burned."

"No, he didn't sustain significant burns. Oh good, here's Dr. Amarti," she said and waived over a tiny older woman. If I held my arm up and out, Dr. Amarti could've stood under it and not touched her head to my arm. She had delicate features, and that beautiful complexion and carriage that made it impossible to guess her age.

"Mr. Jennings, I'm Dr. Sylvia Amarti. I've been treating Mr. Jacobs since he was brought in. I understand you're his medical contact and have his power of attorney and can make his medical decisions?" she asked while she firmly herded me to a small room near the row of patient cubicles.

"That's right," I said, "and please call me Mark. *(Brian is a person. See him.)* Brian is my partner. I have all the paperwork in this file. Please, tell me what's going on. Why can't I see him?"

Dr. Armati shared a look with Emily and girded herself. "Mr. Jacobs came into the ER suffering a prolonged grand mal seizure, and we weren't able to stop him from seizing. I tried Dilantin, but it was useless. Thank goodness he was wearing his medical alert bracelet and we were able to call his neurologist and consult. Dr. Baron will be here shortly, and you can speak with him yourself."

"Go on," I said and braced myself for whatever was coming. This shitstorm.

"The prolonged seizure caused Mr. Jacobs to suffer temporary loss of oxygen to his brain. That, combined with the smoke he inhaled before he was pulled from the vehicle, made it necessary to intubate him. Do you understand?" she paused.

"Yes, he's on a respirator," I whispered.

("She can stay alive for a time on artificial support. Every time she slips back and forth from the coma state it weakens her body, and one of these times she won't come back at all. I can tell you, it is painful on her body. I can't tell you what to do, and it takes strength to let go.")

"Yes. Mr. Jennings." I looked sharply at her. "Mark. His condition was beginning to stabilize. But, well, the brain is a funny organ, Mark," she said. She paused and actually reached out and touched my elbow. I was barely aware of it. All I could hear was the rush of blood in my ears and the screams that threatened to drown her out. Why couldn't she hear the screaming?

(Dad and I looked at each other and he nodded. We'd already had this conversation. With Mom. It would be hard on the rest of the family, but it was done. We couldn't let her suffer any more.)

"Whether it was the accident, the smoke inhalation, the length of the initial seizure, or any number of factors, his brain will not stop triggering seizures. The complication, as you know, is the tumor. It may be that it's invaded a part of the brain that controls muscular activity. The CAT scan shows significant growth from last month, and serious damage to all surrounding areas," she said.

"Oh God. Not now. Not today. I'm not ready, Dr. Amarti. Please tell me not now," I begged. She did what no other doctor we had been to see did. This tiny china doll of a woman pulled my six foot-plus frame into her arms and shushed me like a child.

"Mark, I'm controlling any pain he might be having. He regains consciousness at moments, but that will be fading. I'm so sorry, but your young man is not going to make a recovery. I'll go over the options available for his care, and you have a serious choice to make. Shhh." This goddess continued to hold me in her arms.

The world fractured. Exploded. The shrapnel was lodged in every square inch of me and nobody but this kind woman saw it. And that's what allowed me to pull myself together and take care of Brian.

(I told the doctor. "Dad and I made the call already. She's coming home. We can't let this go on any longer. She wants to die at home and we'll let her." He looked at us and nodded. His eyes were bright. "I admire your strength. Not every family can do what is right. Bless you. For her sake.")

This man was the husband of my heart. I'd be a man for him, the man he deserved.

I SAT in a chair beside his bed, holding his hand. The noises of all the machinery that monitored him and kept him breathing didn't register.

All I saw was him, all I heard was his voice, all I breathed was his smell.

(How he looked the first time we made love. When I asked him to be mine. When he told me he loved me for the first time.)

I waited. I watched. His body would jump and muscles would twitch and jerk.

(When we got the diagnosis of the tumor. When his body started to betray him. When we couldn't make love anymore in case he had a seizure.)

The doctor stood there with me. We were just waiting. I couldn't do this until he was awake for a minute. I needed to see his eyes one more time.

Finally, his eyes flickered open and he blinked and searched, tried to focus. I squeezed his hand and drew his attention to me. He looked up and his eyes widened. His mouth tried to move, to speak, but the tube wouldn't allow it.

(When he passed out from a seizure the first time. When I found him unconscious on the bathroom floor. When I left home that morning.)

"Shh. Sweet, sweet baby. I'm here with you. I won't let you go through this all by yourself. Remember, we talked about this. I know you can see me, and hear me."

He looked up, his gaze locked on mine and understanding flooded his eyes. He gripped at my hand as muscle tremors jerked parts of his body. I held it hard so he would know I had him.

(When we decided not to have the surgery that could leave him in a vegetative state. When we told Dad and he cried, holding Brian. When he called him his son.)

"I know you were looking for Robbie. It's okay. Don't worry about him. It's just you and me here. I wanted to see those beautiful eyes of yours one more time, baby. I'm ready. Are you ready?"

Relief flooded his eyes. A single tear started to run down the side of his face. I bent down and kissed it away. I put my mouth right next to his ear so he could hear me. "My love. My life. My husband. It's been my great honor to love you and I only hope I was worthy of it."

(When I first met him at Ryan's party. When we started dating. When I realized I loved him.)

He jerked a little at that and leaned his head toward my ear. I could hear a moan in his throat.

"Shh. We had a good life together. I'll miss you every day for the rest of my life. You're my heart and it'll go with you. I'll be here, and I'll hold your hand, and you focus on me, and when you leave me, you won't be alone. Don't be afraid. We won't be saying good-bye, baby. Just, 'til later.'"

I leaned back and nodded to the doctor. She started shutting down the respirator, and the noise stopped. All that was left was the heart monitor.

(When he cheated. When he left me. When I knew he would leave me again.)

I climbed beside him into the cold, sterile bed and wrapped my arms around him and turned his head to mine so as he left this life, he could see my love for him.

I kept talking and telling him he was loved and singing his favorite song, this song that broke my heart every time I heard it and I couldn't fix him or guide him home, until the monitor stopped beeping. Dr. Amarti turned it off before the alarm could sound, took her stethoscope and listened to his chest for a moment. Nodding, she turned to leave. But before she did, she turned and stood behind me, placed one hand over my heart, and hugged me from behind.

Then she slipped out of the room and closed the curtain behind her, leaving me with Brian. I kept humming in his ear even though I was there alone. Lights *will* guide you home, love.

(When he is gone. When I am alone. When the lights go out.)

CHAPTER FOURTEEN

WE'D decided on low-key for his memorial service. I supposed it helped, the knowing in advance, but honestly, the marking time in a sort of hellish limbo also let me think that it really wasn't going to happen. So Brian and I had already planned it out, and all I had to do was contact the funeral home, and then ask our friend Janet to sing. He always loved her voice. We'd both wanted to be cremated so there'd only be a memorial service in the chapel, no viewing and graveside service.

I'd sat down with Todd and arranged for a three months leave of absence. If he hadn't agreed, I was prepared to quit. The thought of going to work, not seeing Robbie, not having Brian to come home to, I just couldn't do it. He agreed.

The day of the service was one of those days we sometimes get in summer in Atlanta. The air was dry, the temperature moderate. The sky was clear. The service was set for two in the afternoon in the chapel of the funeral home we'd used when we buried Mom. I'd spent an hour or so sitting in the private family room with Dad. I just stared and waited for time to start the service.

The door opened and someone came in. I didn't have the energy to turn and see who. I felt, more than heard, someone standing right behind me. "The service starts at two. Everybody'll be in the chapel. I'll see you in there," I said flatly.

A tentative voice whispered, "Mr. Mark? Is it okay if I'm in here?"

"Robbie," I said. It was all I could manage to get out. And I turned around.

"Mr. Mark, I'm so sorry. I liked Mr. Brian and I just heard about this," his voice trailed off, unsure. I was off the chair and had him in a tight hug before he got the last words out. He stiffened at first, but then he relaxed and reached up and hugged me back. After a minute I pulled him back.

"Where've you been?" I asked. "I've been so worried, Robbie." He looked down at his shoes and scuffed them around and mumbled for a minute. Started and stopped and hemmed and hawed, then looked back at me.

"Is it okay if I stay for the funeral? If you let me, I promise I won't run off," he said. When he looked up, fear and hope fought for control of his face. "If you still want to see me later. If you don't, I'll go and leave you alone and not bother you anymore," he whispered.

"Don't you fucking dare," I warned him. "You can stay and then come over to my house after the service. We're all having an early dinner there. I want you there, do you understand? Tell me you'll come see me after we're finished here."

"Okay, Mr. Mark, I promise," he said, with relief.

"The chapel's next door. Why don't you go in there and sit down and wait, okay? It won't be long," I walked him over to the connecting door. He nodded and went without saying anything else.

"Who was that boy?" my dad asked. I'd forgotten he was there, in my relief.

"Dad, that was Robbie. He's the boy that I was telling you about. He ran away from where I work. Brian was out looking for him when…." The grief was never far from the surface. Grief and anger and hurt.

"When he wrecked," Dad finished for me, his face so compassionate. "Brian made that choice to be out driving, son. He knew what could happen. He wanted to find that boy and make sure he was safe too. It wasn't his fault, Mark. If it wouldn't have been then, it would've been soon. You heard what the doctor said, the tumor was growing again." He reached out and pulled me into his arms. "I know it hurts, son, but you have to let him go today. It's just his body we're saying good-bye to, you know. He's like your momma, he's always going to be in your heart. And you'll see him again. Just like I'll see your mom. But don't you forget you still have a lot of time left, boy. Grieve for him, but don't you fucking dare give up," he said into my ear.

Having my dad hold me in his strong arms like when I was a boy finally, finally allowed me to let go. It was like being told that I could fall apart now, that my daddy would keep me in one piece. Sometimes you are never too old to be held by a parent. He just held on and rocked me just like he did when I was a baby. Just like I did for him when his love died.

I loved this man. He was able to keep going on. Maybe I could too.

THE service was… amazing.

I was expecting my family, a few of our friends, and maybe a couple of people from work to be there. What I walked into was a chapel so full there were people that stood in the back since all the seating was taken.

My entire family was there. Antonio and Jason, and Robbie, who was sitting with them. And people from my job. Kids. Dan and a whole crew of people from my last agency. Ryan and his partner Jake—Brian and I met at their party. And people I didn't recognize, some of whom must have been men and women who worked with Brian over the years. Even classmates of mine from college.

We kept it really simple and brief. There was a pastor Brian and I had known through the AIDS ministry that I'd asked to do a small reading and prayer. Janet sang "Amazing Grace." Then I stood to talk. If I nothing else, I could offer this last thing to my lover.

"Thank you all for coming today. Brian'd be so happy and shocked to see how many people were here to say good-bye to him. But it doesn't surprise me."

"You all know Brian was a loving and giving man. He didn't have any family to speak of. When I met him, God, it seems like yesterday, I thought, 'What a strange guy.' He was so good-looking and funny, but when I saw him the first time, he was just standing there against a wall and looking out at everybody having fun, and I asked my buddy Ryan, 'Who is that guy?'"

"'He's a friend of Jake's; I think his name's Brian.' So I went over and just stood next to him for a minute, you know, to size him up, and then said hello to him and 'I'm Mark' and all that.

"He did the funniest thing. He pointed with his cup at some girl that was chatting up Jake and kind of hanging onto his arm and looking up at him with big old doe eyes, and he said, 'Barking up the wrong tree, don't you think?' And then he laughed."

"And you know what he sounded like when he laughed. Jesus, like the sun coming out. I knew right then that we were going to be friends.

"Then I ended up taking him to Sunday breakfast at my mom and dad's house and he just, God, he just soaked it up and couldn't get enough of the way Mom kind of took him under her wing and made him one of her kids.

"I think that's when I started falling in love with Brian Jacobs. When I saw how hungry he was for love and family and somebody who wanted him. Y'all know that us being together came later, and we had some tough times like every couple does, but I never stopped loving that man.

"And now I have to say good-bye to him today," and with that my voice broke a little. My eyes got a little swimmy, and then I felt Dad step up and put his arm around my shoulders.

"I'm glad you all came here today. He'd have been so happy to have family and friends around him. And he'd say to all of us, 'Don't be sad.'"

"He wrote it down, you know. What he wanted me to tell everyone that came today." And I pulled a card from my jacket.

"'Brian's rules for today. Hug as many people as you can. Tell something funny about me. Say 'I love you' to the person you want to know it. Don't cry. Remember it's okay to laugh. And last, but not least'," and I couldn't do it, and had to hand the card to my dad.

"'Last but not least'," he read, "'remind Mark I loved him best and most.'"

Janet stood one more time and sang his last requested song.

"At last my love has come along, my lonely days are over…"

FINALLY, almost everyone was gone. I sent them all back over to the house to eat some of the food everybody kept dropping off. Say what you will about us Southerners and gay men, we know how to do a funeral right. Patty said she'd coordinate things for me so I could have a little time alone. And I really needed to talk to Robbie.

When I found him, he was outside on the lawn sitting with Jason, playing some kind of handheld video game. They had their heads together and were talking up a storm. Antonio was on a bench watching them. I didn't know whether to talk to him first or to Robbie. But when Antonio stood up and came over to me, I really didn't have much choice.

"God, Mark, I'm so sorry about all this, man," he said into my ear after he pulled me into a big hug. "That was a beautiful service. Me and Jason, this is the first time he's been to a funeral and I was kind of worried. He really loves you and he's been so worried about you and asking about you all the time."

He squeezed me tight and kissed the side of my head, then let me go and pulled back to look at me. "I found him for you, just like I promised. I fucking owe you and this was the least I could do for you," he said and nodded at Robbie.

"*You* found him? How? When?" I sputtered.

He told me how he had gotten his friend Mario to come up from Florida and search all the hangouts he knew from living on the street. How they hit pay dirt and were able to find Zev, the bastard he was staying with. And how they had lain in wait until he could catch Robbie alone and fill him in on what had happened.

I pulled Antonio into a hug, letting him know silently how much that meant to me and how grateful I was to him. He held me tight and let his care and friendship for me fill the moment. I closed my eyes and just breathed him in. He really had come to mean so much to me, and this, this was a gift.

"How'd you get him to come with you? You saw what he was like last time," I said when I let him go. He looked over at the boys. At Robbie. And he got this incredibly soft look on his face.

"Mark, the boy lost his shit. Cried like a baby. I didn't know if it was from the drugs he's been on or if he was really feeling it. I told him I'd help him get cleaned up. He's been over at my place, and he hasn't had anything. Done anything," he said. "Jason's been staying with me and the two of them, they're getting to be friends. I think it's been good for Robbie to have someone closer to his age to talk to."

I was relieved but I didn't know what the fuck to do next. Robbie couldn't stay with Antonio. And I couldn't let him go back to that scumbag that was using him. Maybe... "Let's get back to my house. There's food and I have an idea. You bring him and Jason along, okay?" I asked.

Antonio went over and talked to them for a minute, and I saw Robbie look over at me and say something. Whatever he heard back seemed to be good enough, and the three of them got up and started toward the parking lot. He looked back for a minute, and I nodded to him and gave him a smile.

When they all were gone, I got in my car and sat for a minute. Breathed in and out a few times. This was my new life. I could do this. I just hoped that one day, maybe soon, breathing wouldn't hurt so much.

THANKFULLY, most people went on home after the service. I'm not sure my poor house could've held everybody, but Patty was an angel. She'd come in sometime that day and set up chairs and cleaned up and made the place ready for me. And there she was, setting food out as she managed the family and friends that did make it. She caught my eye when I came in and I mouthed *I love you* to her. Her eyes were so soft and full of love and loss too. She'd loved Brian from the first day she met him.

The first thing I had to do was go find Dad. When I found him I pulled him into our... *my* bedroom and we sat down on the bed so I could talk to him.

Why did it take me so long to remember where I came from? The strength I had behind me, and the love. All the time I could've leaned on my dad, and I thought I had to do it all by myself. Fix things myself. Just made me realize that what I was going to ask was the right thing to do.

"Are you okay, son? I know today was rough, but just remember we're all here for you. Me and your brothers and sisters. Anything we can do, Mark, anything at all," he said. I took a deep breath.

"Well, Dad, it's funny you ask," I started. And then I told him about Robbie, and how Antonio found him. How he was gay and self-hating and thought nobody would want him. About the drugs and the sex and prostitution. We just sat there and looked at each other for a minute. I picked at a thread on the comforter. I was almost afraid to ask. And then he surprised me.

"He'll come home with me. He can have your old room 'til we figure things out," he said like it was a given. "That boy needs to know a real family doesn't throw their kids away. You're gay and you turned out pretty fucking good. If I do say so myself."

He looked at me with determination. "When he gets here, let's the three of us talk, okay? I'll make sure this boy has a home, son. You know your mother and me were licensed with the state for emergency placements; all I have to do is call them Monday and talk to the supervisor. Yeah, this is a fucked-up situation, but they owe me one after all the favors we did them. They can stretch the rules to make it happen. If you and Brian thought enough of him to worry and look for him when he ran off, there has to be something good about him. Just come and get me."

He slowly got up and looked around. Saw the pictures of the Brian and me, smiling and happy. With Mom and him at Christmas. Brian with the dogs as they tumbled around on the floor. He shook his head slowly.

"I'm going to miss that boy."

WE WENT back out to the kitchen, where we always seemed to congregate. Well, those of the family who liked to pick at the food and gossip. So yeah, I went there first. Looked for Antonio and the boys there.

But before I could get over to them, I felt someone touch my arm. When I turned it was my brother, Sam. I'd caught glimpses of him over the past few days, but he'd stayed back and I was fucking glad. I didn't have the stomach for his bullshit.

"Mark, can I talk to you for a second?" he asked.

I looked and saw the guys talking, and he saw where I glanced and said, "Just for a minute, okay?" I reluctantly nodded and we stepped into the hallway.

"What do you want, Sam?" I said bluntly. He swallowed visibly, and I could see what looked like confusion and something else I hadn't seen before cross his face. It looked like compassion and, fuck him, love.

"Mark, I know I've said some really shitty things to you and Brian over the years," he started.

"Yeah," I said, not sure what he was going to say.

He looked down and cleared his throat. When he looked back up, there were tears shining in his eyes. "I know it probably doesn't mean anything coming from me, but I'm sorry as hell about what happened. If it'd been me and Jean," and he shook his head, "I just don't know if I could've handled it like a man like you've been doing. I'm sorry." And he reached out to touch my arm again.

I didn't know what to say, and didn't know that I believed him. But for Brian's sake, I'd bury the hatchet down today. Not to say I wouldn't pick it back up if he started shit again. But for today, it was enough. "Thanks," I said quietly. He nodded and walked off. I shook my head and went back into the kitchen.

Robbie looked a little lost and was hanging close to Jason. I don't know if it was the situation, the number of people hanging out, or what. But I know my family can be overwhelming to people not used to the noise and sheer numbers. I nodded at them.

"Hey guys, thanks for coming over. Jason, buddy, you hungry? Robbie? There's all kinds of munchies and stuff here. Antonio, grab—" Before I could get the words out, Patty swooped in and took over, as older sisters are liable to do.

"And who're these big fellas?" she asked. "Mark, introduce me to these handsome young men." I rolled my eyes. And she liked to call *me* a flirt? She's such a mom. And today she was my goddamned hero.

"Patty, this is my friend Antonio and his son, Jason. And this is Robbie. He's a young man I know through work," I told her.

I grabbed her up in my arms and swallowed her up in a bear hug and gave her a big old Jennings kiss. "And this crazy lady is my sister, Patty. She took care of me today and got everything set up nice. And she may have even baked that big old red velvet cake over there."

She glared at me. Looked me up and down and didn't like what she saw, I could tell. I knew I hadn't been eating or sleeping much and looked like hell. Patty was such a mom that she forgot sometimes she was my sister. Damn but I loved her. "Well Mark, they look like they're starving. And you, little brother, eat! Come on boys, fill those plates up and I'll get you something to drink. Coke? Tea? Antonio?"

I let her get them all settled in and fed, and I picked at the Honeybaked ham and cheese plate. I hoped to hell she was planning on sending some of this shit home with everybody, because it wouldn't fit in my fridge. And really, I hadn't been all that hungry. It would just go bad. She gave me a look, though, and I ate.

As things tended to do, the conversations drifted in and out and around and people went from one group to another. Pretty soon everybody'd been over to say a kind word or squeeze my shoulder until I thought I'd be permanently bruised. But I saw an opening and took it. I caught Antonio's eye and looked quickly down at Robbie and jerked my head toward the back of the house. He damn well better be able to read the gesture.

"Robbie? Buddy, is it okay if we go and talk for a minute? I haven't had time to say boo to you yet. Want to come and let me show you the rest of the house?" I asked.

He looked around and Antonio gave him a little nod, so he got up, said something in Jason's ear, and came with me. I showed him around, mostly to put him at ease. Poor guy looked like he was afraid I was going to throw him out the door or something. We went into my bedroom, and I knew no one would follow me in there, so I'd have a chance to talk to him.

I motioned for him to sit in one of the chairs I had next to the bay windows. I sat down in the other and looked over at him. "How're you doing, Robbie?" I started.

"I'm okay, Mr. Mark. I wanted to come see you when Antonio told me about what happened, but, um, I needed to take care of a couple of things first," he said. "I'm really, really sorry about Mr. Brian." He looked ready to either puke or run.

"Robbie," and I was really, really careful here, "it's okay. I know what's going on, and I would've been to see you sooner, but well, we both had things we had to take care of, didn't we?" I told him what'd happened with Brian. How I'd been searching for him.

"It's okay, Mr. Mark. And I know," he gulped and got a little teary, "I know Mr. Brian was looking for me when, when…." And then the tears did spill over. Fuck. That's what all this rabbit bullshit was.

"Robbie, I don't blame you. Brian had a brain tumor and was dying. He wouldn't have made it much longer." I bulldozed through so it wouldn't hurt so much. "It's okay. But I want to talk about you, buddy. I want you to be safe. Okay? Because I really couldn't take it if something happened to you too after all this."

He waited a minute, took it all in. The fear and dread I had seen on his face was replaced with confusion. And determination. "But Zev'll be looking for me, and he won't like it if I don't come back. He's not really nice when he's mad," he said and trembled a little.

Fuck. That. Bastard. I wanted to see that fucker in jail. After about fifteen minutes with me and a baseball bat.

"Robbie, I'm going to cut straight to the chase here, okay? I don't want you using anymore, and I don't want you to sell yourself ever again. If I can offer you something else, somewhere else to stay," and saw the look I knew was coming, saw his fear and moved to head it off. "Somewhere *not* the Hope House. Would you stay?"

He looked a little suspicious, now that he knew I wasn't talking about him going back there. "Where're you talking about?" he asked. Time to go for broke. And I filled him in on what my dad was offering. A home. Safety. A family.

"Are you serious?" he whispered. His eyes were round and wide open and his face was a little pale. I leaned forward in my chair so I could be right up in his face.

"I've already talked to him about it. There'll be rules and no drugs. Robbie, you know I'd let you live with me, but I'd have to leave my job, and well…." I stalled for a second and took in a deep breath, "I just lost Brian, Robbie. I need some time to grieve him. By myself. You understand, don't you?"

"Mr. Mark, that would mean we'd be almost… brothers," he said. The look of awe and hope about undid me.

"So what do you say, bud? You want to talk to my dad?" I asked gently.

He just looked at me and nodded. Something in me that was clenched loosened a little. And I went and got my dad.

CHAPTER FIFTEEN

November 2005

I WONDERED why the hell I'd ever thought having a phone with a cord was a good idea. All it did was make moving around the kitchen awkward and conversations a bitch to keep focused on. When I pulled bagged salad out of the fridge and tried to take lasagna out of the oven *and* talk to Antonio all at the same time, I ran out of hands and had to balance the receiver on my shoulder.

"If it wasn't for Robbie pitching a fit, I wouldn't even be going to the family Thanksgiving this year. I can't do that to him though. Leaving him alone to deal to that bunch of lunatics would have him running for the hills before dessert." I laughed. Damn, but the pasta smelled good.

"He'll be okay, and you need to be there. You know Patty'll hunt you down if you try to blow off dinner. At least you won't be eating deli turkey and chips," he moaned.

"Don't you have Jason?" I cooked way too much of this shit, I thought. It's hard to gauge cooking for one.

"No, his mom and stepdad are taking him to Orlando for the week. Just me. How's Robbie doing? I know him and Jason talk all the time on the phone, but he won't tell me shit."

"Yeah, I know. Dad says he's always on the phone with him. But he seems to be good. He's in school. The social worker's still making home visits it seems like every damn week. Dad raised six kids, and I think he knows a thing or two about what works and what doesn't. And he raised a gay one so Robbie isn't throwing him any curveballs," I ranted.

"You know that's not what that shit is about," he chided. "It's them looking out for him because of the drugs and all the other stuff. They'd have him back in a group home or some shit if they didn't think your dad's place was good for him."

"You're right, damn it. Hey, what're you doing right now?" I asked.

No way was I going to eat all this. Leftovers for lunch and dinner tomorrow were way too many carbs, and before I knew it I'd invited him to eat. Told him to get his ass over in the next twenty minutes and help me eat all this crap.

"And bring your table with you," I said.

He was quiet a minute. "You sure? You haven't felt up to having a massage since, well, for a few months. I don't mind, but you sure?"

"Yeah. Nineteen minutes now. Get here," I joked.

"Asshole," he said and hung up.

I grabbed a couple of plates and flatware out of the cabinet and set the table in the dining room. Then I thought about it and found a bottle of red wine and two glasses. *No* fucking ice. As I moved around and got things ready and watched the clock for when to take the bread out, I kept hearing a funny noise in the house.

Five months in the house alone and I was losing my fucking mind. When Brian'd moved out when we were split up, the house was quiet. Now though, man, it was too much some nights. I couldn't watch shit on television, and music still hurt too much. Too raw. With Lucy and Ricky living with Dad now—actually with Robbie, since he loved the dogs and they reminded me too much of Brian—I thought I'd gotten used to the silence.

The timer dinged and I popped the bread in a basket, set it with everything else on the table, and eyed the clock again. Everything looked and smelled great, but what the fuck was that noise? Then I realized it was me, humming.

I really didn't have time to think about it too much before Antonio knocked on the door. He took the massage table into the den. He sniffed and made yummy-yummy noises. I heard his stomach growl, and when I teased him about it, he wrestled me into the dining room.

We made light conversation over dinner and polished off the bottle of wine, and I opened another one. It was Friday and I didn't have to work the next day, so I could relax. I'd missed this a lot, hanging out with Antonio and just shooting the shit. I hadn't seen him but maybe five or six times since July, and that was when he called and demanded we have lunch. The funeral had been tough as hell. I felt like days just went by and I didn't notice. I knew things were going on and life was happening, but I wasn't really a participant.

Five long months, a hundred and fifty short days.

I hadn't been able to feel right in my skin. The world was just a little grayer. And for all the friends and family telling me, "Time will make it better," and my personal favorite, "God works in mysterious ways," well, the best thing I can say about it is they meant well.

Of course my sister Brenda, she of Sister Mary Vagina fame, wasn't talking to me much these days. I loved her because I had to, but to try to tell me just two weeks after Brian's death "God has a plan, and it's not ours to know it" didn't sit real well with me.

"Tell me, Bren, if you got a call telling you Frank and the kids just got killed in a wreck, how would you feel about God's fucking plan? You'd just go quietly about your business because they're in a better place or some shit? You fucking sit there and tell me how it'd feel if I told you some lame-ass shit like that when you've lost everything *you* loved.

"When you've got something real to say to me that isn't something you think is appropriate for a nice little Christian girl to say, and don't we fucking know better than *that*, when you can be my fucking sister and think about *me* for a fucking change, then you come talk to me."

"But until then, you just fucking stay the hell away from me. Don't call. Don't write. Don't email. I don't want to hear from you until… just until." I was so mad I was breathless. Then I hung up on her.

Damn, the anger had lit me up, and I felt something. Almost alive for a minute while the adrenaline burned through my body. Then it melted away, and I just felt sick.

Was I cruel? Maybe. Did I regret it? Not for one damned second. And there were other tensions in the family right then too. Dad's decision to foster Robbie went over like a lead balloon with the God Squad and the Asshole. Funny about their family values. Now I'd given them some more ammunition against me. Just, fuck 'em.

Family. Can't change 'em, can't feed 'em to the lions. Gotta love 'em.

But today I felt a little more like myself.

Afterward, we cleaned up, and yes, I made his Italian ass wash plates and help me scrub out the lasagna pan. We joked around some more and flopped down on the sofa with the second bottle of wine. I'd been drinking most of it myself and knew Antonio was watching how much he'd had since he was driving. At his house, I usually was the one having just one glass. I didn't miss his glances at my glass and how I kept filling it. But I was having too much fun to care.

"Thanks for coming over and eating. There just isn't an easy way to make meals for one. Can't be done," I said.

"Sure there is, you just got to portion it in smaller dishes and freeze it. But I much prefer this solution." He rubbed his belly. I watched him and noticed more definition in his abs than I remembered.

"Shit, you been working out every day or something?" I asked. He wasn't small, with his wrestler's build, but he was always really nicely muscled, not ripped. Not like what I saw there now, and I reached over and knocked on them with my knuckles. He laughed and shoved my hand away.

"Business's been slow so I'm hitting the gym every day. It's been a while since you went with me, but that's cool. I'm doing more of the computer stuff now anyway. I'll have to show you. Started designing custom workstations and tinkering around with how to work some caseless circuits and neon and fans. This shit is the wave of the future, Mark. If I can just figure out how to keep the dust out, and then fit the components into a handcrafter frame, there'll be people knocking my fucking door down to buy these things. I'm getting closer, but all the things I need to do this right just aren't on the market yet," he rambled on.

I was clueless and not really paying attention as I poured us both the last of the wine left in the bottle. He kept saying something about motherboards and sound cards and processor speed. I kind of just watched his face and his hands move around. He was really dorky and nerdy-looking and all intense when he got wound up about computers. I laughed to myself.

"Are you even paying attention to me anymore, buddy? Or has the wine got you? You want me to go on home and you can go to bed?" he asked. That woke me up some.

"No!" I said probably a little too loudly. "No, man," I took it down a notch, "I'm having too good a time right now. And we haven't hung out that much lately. I needed this. Needed to do something again."

I rolled my head on the back of the couch and looked at him. "Man, I'm sorry I've been such a bad friend," I started to apologize.

He reached over and pushed my head. "Mark, shut the fuck up. It ain't about who's been a good friend or any bullshit like that. Five months is still fresh. You miss him, man, I know. I can't imagine going through what you did, losing the person you love the most like that. If I ever lost Jason," his voice cracked a little and he shook his head, "or you. Damn, Mark, I owe you so much. You helped me out when nobody else would. I don't know why you hang around with an asshole like me anyway. You know what I do every day, what a struggle it is to make ends meet. You deserve better." He pulled me over and shifted us sideways a little, my back against his chest.

He put his arms around me and rubbed my chest with those big, strong hands of his. "But it ain't about me. It's about you. You just needed some time and some space. Man, what kind of asshole would I've been not to let you have it? Let me take care of you here, okay? I ain't going anywhere."

His hands were so nice on my chest and belly, and he made smaller and smaller circles on me.

"Don't you go anywhere either, baby," he whispered. He kissed the back of my head and hugged me against him tight. He leaned back against the arm of the couch, and I slid in between his legs, back still against his chest.

It felt really nice to lie there against him like that. The wine and food made me a little drowsy, and I snuggled into the V of his legs and shifted up on the couch. I pulled his arms around me and laid my head on his neck. The wine, I thought, I must be a little more drunk than I thought, and he must be too. But it felt nice to be held again. Even if it was Antonio and not Brian.

When I rubbed my cheek against his jaw and sighed a little, he sucked in a lungful of air and held it for a minute. As relaxed as I was, I noticed it but didn't give it much weight. He let out his breath and pulled me against him really tight. I felt him brushing light kisses down my ear and neck. The feeling of safety and peace, that beautiful feeling I'd been missing all these months, was right there in that moment.

I turned my head around and up to him, and looked at him through eyes barely open. His lips grazed against mine, and I felt him smile. How funny, I thought. He kissed me. I smiled and lay back down against his chest and dozed off.

WHEN I woke up I wasn't sure for a minute where I was, and in my disoriented and half-buzzed state, I thought Brian was the one laying there with me. So I stretched, groped him, and chuckled a little. But the body didn't feel anything like what it should have. Beefier, more muscles, even the smell was different. I opened my eyes and saw my hand was on Antonio's package.

Holy fuck, what was I doing?

I snatched my hand back and fell on the floor when I tried to get up off the couch. I started to remember what the hell was going on and where I was about then, and didn't know whether to be embarrassed, ashamed, or angry. All of those emotions ran around in my head.

I was so disgusted at myself I didn't know what to say. How the hell could I be putting my hands on another man, especially *Antonio*, who was being such a good friend to me? Was I that big of an ass, that fucked-up, that I was all horn-dogged over my straight best friend? And right here in mine and Brian's home too, just a few months after losing him?

Some of those dark emotions must have showed on my face because Antonio, who must have woken when I flopped so gracefully on the floor, turned pale and started to stammer and apologize. "God, Mark, I'm so sorry, man. I didn't mean to fall asleep like that and, shit, I don't know what happened."

"Don't worry about it, man. I just… I better just go take a shower and go to bed." And I couldn't even look him in the eyes. All I could do was shake my head.

He got up very carefully, and I saw him start to reach out toward me, and I flinched a little. His hand stilled and he took a couple of steps back, then went to the den where he had left his table. He picked it up by the handle and walked to the front door.

"Mark," he started, "I…." I looked up and he shook his head and opened the door. "I'm so sorry, man." And I knew I heard tears in his voice and real pain. But I was so wrapped up in mine I couldn't make myself do anything about it, and he closed the door and left.

I just sat there on my knees, trying to get up enough energy to get into the bedroom. Finally I did, and crawled under the covers, clothes and all. I just laid there, curled in a ball and looked at the shadows cast across the room. I wondered what to do, how to fix this thing that was going on with me.

Where did I go wrong? Was it that I forgot what Brian meant to me, how much I'd lost? I knew there was no question of my love for him, or his for me. Was it just too soon to try to be normal again? What the fuck were the rules?

I knew how to grieve for friends, because God knows I'd lost enough of them in my life. AIDS, suicides, accidents. I even learned the slow scabbing over of the heart when I lost my mom. But nobody tells you how you're supposed to act or feel when your other half's gone. How long it takes 'til the hole there starts to maybe fill in some.

Or maybe it never does get better and that's why they don't tell you. Maybe you just walk around, do all the *doing* stuff, and pretend that you're okay until either you lie down and don't get back up, or you believe it. Like some kind of half-life or something.

Part of me wanted to be okay again. Be normal, whatever the fuck that was. Okay, I knew what some of it was. It was having dinner, making jokes, getting a little drunk, and not getting your guts ripped out when you remembered you weren't supposed to be having fun. It was hanging out with your best friend. It was being touched again, for fuck's sake.

I'd read about a study one time where scientists said the average human being needed to be touched by another person something like ten times a day. That people who were deprived of touch, not conversation, not food, just simple human touch, could and would go insane after an extended period of time.

Was five months enough? Was I on the downhill slope to crazy town? Was that why it felt so good and so, so safe and right when Antonio held onto me?

I owed him a lot. He was trying to be the kind of friend who was patient and didn't pass judgment. Who didn't treat me like I was made of fucking glass and would break, or ignored it and tried to be all fake cheery. Here I went and shit all over that, made him feel weird, and that just wasn't right.

He deserved better than to have been felt up and laid all over like some cheap date. He didn't seem to mind it, I know, but he had as much wine as I did and fuck, it wasn't like we didn't almost cuddle sometimes anyway. I had to smile, and thought about how his buddies from the street would give him shit for hanging with me like we did. But then the guilt hit me and I remembered how hurt he looked when he left.

All because I couldn't keep my fucking hands to myself.

I decided I'd call him the next day and try to apologize. Maybe even get him to come to Thanksgiving dinner at Dad's house. He wouldn't say no to a chance to see Robbie.

Yeah, that sounds good, I thought, and drifted off to sleep.

CHAPTER SIXTEEN

Thanksgiving 2005

"ALL right, bitches, move away from the turkey and keep your hands where I can see 'em," I shouted into the gaggle of family that took up all the space in the kitchen. I brought in the dressing and saw that Patty and Robert's wife, Jennifer, had pulled the foil back and were pinching little bits of goodness off the bird.

I heard giggling and looked around and there was Robbie, standing back like he usually did when there was a crowd of Jennings around. But at least he looked relaxed and not so worried about being noticed.

"Hey Robbie, buddy, how about going out to my car and bringing in the box of drinks in the back seat for me, okay?" I asked.

"Will do, Mark," he said and ran outside.

"At least he doesn't call you *Mister Mark* anymore." Patty laughed and slapped me on the arm. "It was tough getting all the kids to stop trying to call me Mrs. Patty."

"But you look like such a Mrs. Patty. Elementary school librarian. Lunch lady. Spooky old witch in the haunted house. Miiiissssuuuuss Paattttyyyy...." I played, then ducked the slap aimed at the back of my head.

"You're in a good mood. How're you doing? What's going on?" she asked around the mob of kids that came running through the kitchen and out the door. I unpacked the dressing and put it in the oven to keep warm. As many as were already here, the whole family wasn't completely here yet.

I shrugged. "Okay. Some good days, some not so good. Finally got my hands back around things at work. The temp guy did okay on the accounting side, but you know how it is. I like things my own way and it felt weird having somebody's shit on my computer." She knew how funny I was about that.

"Oh, and this guy was—" I looked around and leaned in because of the rugrats everywhere. "—totally a fuck-up. He had straight porn downloaded on my computer. Apparently *somebody* liked women stepping in pudding. Just… shit, Patty, I about pissed in my pants when I opened the files and saw what was there. At least nobody else had access to it. Can you imagine if the kids'd seen that?"

Her eyes were bugged out and she looked about ready to lose it. "Pudding? You. Are. Shitting. Me? Did you keep a backup copy?"

"In my car, on a disc. Remind me to give it to you later," I told her. She loved stupid stuff like that as much as I did. "Oh, and Antonio is coming for dinner." I messed around with the gravy for my dressing, because mine was the best. Really. Just like Mom used to make. She didn't say anything and I finally glanced up and saw she looked at me a little funny.

"What?" I asked.

"You two're good friends, huh?" she said.

"Um, yeah, and remember, Robbie likes him a lot. Trusted him enough to come back with him when Brian died," I said.

"Um-hum."

"What?"

She started to dish out the cranberry relish and made a pickle tray. Kept her hands busy and ignored my look and my question. She had something to say and was trying to figure out how to say it without pissing me off or hurting my feelings. Or the heifer was trying to ignore me. So I did what any red-blooded American man would do and ignored her back, right?

Yeah, not me. I grabbed her and half carried, half pushed her passive-aggressive little ass into the bathroom and closed the door. She sputtered and acted all indignant, but I knew better.

"Spill. I'm not up to playing twenty fucking questions. Now tell me what's on your mind or I'm gonna tell Ray about what *really* happened to his truck and why you and Jennifer had it detailed and sanitized," I threatened. I only knew part of the story, but Ray would never let her in it again.

"You bastard. Bitch. Whatever. A lady doesn't say what I want to call you," she said.

I choked and snorted. "Yeah, you're a real fuckin' lady, Princess Patty. Start talking."

She breathed in a long sigh and looked me in the eye. "You know I love you, little brother, and I'll kick anybody's ass who tries to hurt you. You know that, right?"

The thing was, she meant it. She'd take on anybody she thought might hurt somebody she loved. She reminded me so much of Momma right then and my heart ached a little with missing her still, and then that reminded me of who else wasn't at the table this year. Another time, another year I would've stomped it down and shoved it into a vault, locked it away and not looked at it. This Mark was a little more bruised, a little wiser. A little braver.

I pulled her into a quick hug and whispered my thanks for the reminder of what family does. "But nobody's trying to hurt me, sis. I don't know what you mean. Unless Sam or Brenda have something up their sleeves. And I can handle them," I said, totally confused.

Brenda had prayed on our argument and decided to forgive me, according to all accounts through the family grapevine. As if I cared. I'd forgiven her but would never forget. And Sam seemed… okay, so I wasn't worried about anybody here family-wise. That left Robbie, and Patty loved him. And Antonio.

"What do think Antonio would do to hurt me?" I asked.

"Are you ready for a relationship? I don't know what you're feeling, but I can only imagine how I'd feel if I lost Ray and somebody was after me—"

"What the fuck, Patty? Did you hit the crack pipe or something? Antonio isn't interested in me for a *relationship*! He's my best friend. And darlin', he's more likely to want to get *you* in the sack than me." I laughed. "That man's straight. He talks about women and going down on them and licking girl toes." I shuddered.

"Listen, I know all that. You've told me before all about HetBoy's magic carpet rides, but think about it. Have you heard about any women lately?" she asked. I thought and shook my head no.

"But he's been really sensitive about what we talk about and, you know, tries to not get me upset and thinking about stuff," I said.

"Think, little brother. He's sensitive to *your* moods, *your* words, not mine. As far as we know, he isn't seeing anyone, and from what you told me he hasn't in years. Anyone serious. He mentioned something once to you about being interested in somebody but never told you who. He doesn't mind gay guys, seeing as he's your best friend," she said, ticking all this shit off on her fingers.

"And," she looked up at me and grinned, "he didn't mind a little sumthin' sumthin' with Mr. Happy—at least he didn't mind the one time."

Fuck, I know I turned as red as a fire truck. I never should have told that hussy about what he did the first time I got a massage. I never wanted my sister talking or thinking about me having sex. Unless she was gonna loan me Ray and that tight, tight cowboy-looking ass and then she could talk all she wanted to.

She started up again after I took a breath. "But most of all, Mark," and her voice got really soft, "I see how he *looks* at you when you don't see him looking. He might be straight, but I don't know, maybe his heart knows something his body doesn't yet. And Robbie thinks so too."

Fuck-fuck-*fuck*.

"Do *not* tell me you have been talking about this with that boy? Patty, I'll fucking strangle you. He's fifteen years old for God's sake. What the hell does he know about love?"

"Who said anything about love, sweetheart?" her voice so, so loving and wistful and sad all at the same time. "*That's* why I'm worried. You think about it, okay?"

She opened the door and went back to the kitchen and left me to wonder what the fuck just happened.

WHEN I finally went back out everybody was home and Robbie stood talking to Antonio in the dining room. They picked at the appetizer table that looked ready to collapse from the weight of all the food. I decided to shelve the Antonio question and focus on Robbie. I threw up a hand in greeting to Antonio. He and Robbie both waved back and started talking again.

I went in search of Dad and found him in the family room—that's what we always called the den. The walls were paneled, and two of them were lined with pictures of family. My grandparents, aunts and uncles, brothers and sisters and all their kids. All surrounding a big blown-up candid picture of Mom and Dad taken at some cookout or something. They were facing each other and laughing in the picture, the love between them caught so plainly for everyone to see.

There was a similar picture of all of us kids with our loved ones. I looked at mine and Brian's and felt such a warm rush of memory. We were each holding one of Linda's kids, and they were asleep on our shoulders, and we were walking on the beach holding hands. My sister, in one of the most generous gestures I'd ever seen from her, caught the moment, had it framed and gave a copy to us for my birthday and one to Mom and Dad for the wall.

I noticed a new addition. Robbie sitting on the floor surrounded by my nieces and nephews, playing some kind of game and laughing. His head was thrown back. He looked like a kid without a care in the world. Like a kid *should* look.

The fact that this picture was on the wall said more than all the words my dad could've ever told me about how this was working out. *The Wall* meant you were loved and cared for. And let me tell you, woe be unto the child that moved a single picture. He knew each and every one of them. One time Brenda tried to take down one of her soon-to-be-ex husband. He took her into the bedroom, and we could hear the yelling over the television. The picture was back up before the end of the day.

Dad sat there watching the pregame for whatever football game was coming on. He never liked to hang out in the kitchen, too much noise. He couldn't keep it all straight. He was very hard of hearing and had hearing aids in both ears. They worked well one-on-one, but this family was a bundle of distraction.

I sat down next to him on the couch and slapped him on the thigh. "How's it going, dirty old man?" I asked to make him smile. That's what Mom always called him when he'd tell one of his corny jokes.

"Good. How're you doing, son?" He patted my hand.

"Hangin' in there, Dad, hangin' in there," I told him truthfully. "How's Robbie been?"

His eyes lit up at that. "That boy's doing fine. He's been out in the shed with me messing around building a headboard he wanted." He told me about how Robbie saw it on TV, and the two of them put their heads together, went to the hardware store and the lumber yard and got the stuff and started on it.

He looked at me and smiled his big shit-eating grin. "He's better with the saw and level than you were." My skills with tools were legendary in the family for being disasters. Epic.

"Had any problems out of him?" That was what I really wanted to know.

He shook his head. "He's a good boy. I know he was taking some shit, but let me tell you, son, he mashed his finger with the hammer and I couldn't get him to take anything but an aspirin. He's doing good in school, and I met with his advisor. He's a smart boy. Nobody's ever told him that."

Nothing made my dad madder than a kid who wouldn't try. We didn't have to get all As, and he would take a solid B over a half-assed A anytime. He always knew when we slacked off. He'd dropped out of school to work when his own dad got sick, and he made damn sure we all took our educations seriously.

When I graduated from college, he left the hospital bed the morning after hernia surgery to be there to cheer for me. That meant more to me than the diploma.

"I make him show me his homework every night. I don't know half what that shit is, but I know if he's done it. It's his teacher's job to make sure he understands it, but I can make sure he's trying. And he is," he bragged.

"Mark, I'm gonna tell you something and none of your brothers and sisters know it yet. I've made up my mind but I wanted you to know first. When the social worker clears everything and leaves us the fuck alone, I'm going to adopt him, legally. He doesn't know it yet, and I don't want to get his hopes up until I know for sure the county won't screw this up." He looked at me and asked, "What do you think?"

"I think that's fucking excellent, Dad. Fuck, are you sure?" I said through a huge lump in my throat.

"Mark, I love that boy," he told me, his eyes bright. "All he needs is to know somebody wants him for something besides, well, you know what I'm talking about. For his heart, not what he can do for them. I raised you to know being different is okay, and nothing you could do would make me love you any less. Robbie deserves that too."

I reached over and pulled this fucking amazing man to my side and hugged him. Very quietly, he said, "I think Brian would like that."

My own eyes got fuzzy then. "So do I, Daddy, so do I."

AT LEAST I could relax and enjoy my day with the family knowing Robbie was doing well. Now if I could just get a handle on this thing Patty said was there with Antonio. He sat with me at the second adult table. We had so damn many people there, we always split into the adult table, the second adult table or the cool table, and the kids table. I always managed to get a seat at the cool table.

Patty and Ray sat with us, and Robert and Jennifer, and we managed to fit in one more chair so Robbie could float back and forth between us and the kids. I think he wanted to sit with the kids but thought he'd lose guy points. So of course I led the ragging on him. But I winked and smiled so he knew it was all in fun. That's what family did.

Antonio joked and talked with Ray and Robert. I could see the two wenches as they watched and recorded every word and look. I kicked them both under the table. The second time, Ray jumped and asked what he did wrong when I kicked him by mistake. I rolled my eyes and told him to control his woman. That earned me two sore shins when the "ladies" attacked me together.

I just didn't see it. Antonio was his normal self. He laughed big and hearty, he ate like a dude, and he asked me if I wanted more tea or any dessert. Same stuff he always did. Being a good friend and trying to be nice to me didn't mean he wanted me *that* way.

I made up my mind, though, that I'd be watchful, but all I saw was a great guy. I shrugged to myself and told him, yeah, to get me a piece of the pecan pie. Maybe a little of the banana pudding. While he was there, I *could* use some more tea.

And what the *fuck* was that look between Patty and Jennifer?

CHAPTER SEVENTEEN

August 2006

IT WAS Friday and I decided to take the day off to do some shopping. Part of it was to make it a long weekend, but there was a lot going on, a lot to celebrate and well, just because I wanted to.

It was my birthday, and while I knew I'd be getting a few things, I wanted to look for an iPod for Robbie and thought maybe I'd treat myself to one too. I'd seen more and more guys at the gym strapping one on their arms and listening to tunes when they worked out, and I looked a little retro with my Walkman.

As I walked through Best Buy and wondered which one Robbie'd like better, I thought about how happy he was lately. I planned to take him and Dad out to dinner the next day to celebrate the adoption being final. The judge signed off on it earlier in the week, and I don't think Robbie's feet touched the ground since. Dad was just as damn bad.

The social workers had reduced their visits to monthly beginning in January, and Dad finally sat him down and had *The Talk* with him. He asked me to be there, and poor Robbie was all in knots over what he was sure was going to be bad news. And then, when Dad explained to him what he was going to do and said, "I want you to be my son, like Mark is," well, I'd heard of people melting. I never knew what they meant, but now I did.

The poor kid cried one second and then laughed and hugged Dad for all he was worth the next. "I take it the answer's yes," I said and he flung himself at me too, yelling "Yes!" at the top of his lungs. He bounced around the room and got Lucy and Ricky *way* too excited and wanted to know if he could tell his friends.

I eyed him and asked if there was anybody in particular he wanted to tell. Swear to God I didn't think he could blush after everything he went through in his life, but he did. "Yeah, son, you can go call Jason," Dad told him, and with a quick hug for Dad and a cut of his eyes at me he ran off to his bedroom.

"That went well," I told Dad and he just grinned. "We just need to decide how and when to tell the rest of the family."

The lawyers told him it would be final within six months if nothing went wrong. He didn't really like my idea of waiting to tell them when we left the courthouse after the final paperwork was signed, so we grabbed the speakerphone and started making the calls.

Surprisingly there were no major complaints or bitching. Could be because they knew Dad was there hearing every word, but I liked to think they really liked Robbie. I knew some of them loved him. Having seen Dad and him together at the holidays and the pride the two had over their woodworking skills went a long way toward endearing him to them. We all loved the old man and wanted to see him happy.

We'd even called Robbie's aunt and explained the plans to her. I'd developed a visceral dislike for that woman when I found out she'd refused to take him in the first place, and the conversation we had did nothing to make me like her any more. She was glad she didn't have to do anything other than sign a release of rights as next of kin and started to hang up when I brought up the subject of Robbie having visits with his sister. Her initial flat-out no changed mighty damn quickly when I suggested she might have to answer some questions with the social workers about how she let Robbie end up with a guy who hooked him on drugs and sold him. The first visit took place within a month.

I hadn't seen my dad this happy in a long time. He loved his kids, and being needed. Robbie needed him. They just fit together, and then with Robbie getting into the whole building shit, I gave thanks the whole thing worked out so well.

I paid for everything and headed back out to the mall. I needed to pick up some new clothes: a couple of sweaters and a new lightweight jacket.

After the past year and everything that'd happened I decided I needed—no, *deserved*—a vacation. I bought a ticket to San Francisco for the week of Labor Day, rented a hotel off Union Square, and planned on visiting friends who lived in Marin County for a couple of days. The trip was as spur-of-the-moment as I got and only took Chris and Bill five years of begging and pleading to get me there.

I was getting all my things in order though. When I looked through the closet, I had dressy work stuff, light business casual, and sweats. *When the hell had I become so boring?* I might pick up something nice to wear out to dinner that evening too.

Antonio was taking me out to dinner and wanted to try a new Brazilian steakhouse that opened on Peachtree Street. It was something different and I was looking forward to it. We usually hung out and went to the same old places—The Colonnade or Maria's. When he called and invited me, he told me to dress pretty. And why should I be dressing any differently, I thought?

Ever since Patty'd brought up being careful and was all cryptic, I'd watched Antonio. He was the same guy I'd been hanging out with for years. We listened to music, ate dinner or lunch a couple of times a week, and talked every day on the phone, sometimes twice. Some days maybe three times. But I thought back to all my best friends over the years and that's the same fucking thing we did too. Although, granted, Brian was my best friend and then that became love. But this was Antonio, not Brian.

But Antonio was straight and even though that *one* thing happened all those years ago, he never made a pass or touched my cock or made me think he was interested in me romantically or sexually at all. Well, other than that one kiss. But he was just… experimenting.

After Thanksgiving things were on a more even keel. I'd started hanging out at his place again on Thursdays, and we even started back up with the massages again.

He was very careful the first few times to make sure I was feeling all right, and I finally had to slap his ass when he had me on the table and kept asking, "Are you okay, I'm not making you uncomfortable, am I?" one too many times. He jumped and stuttered a little, which made me laugh. Finally the ice was broken. He acted more like himself and that, more than anything, made me feel right again.

This all changed up our routine some, but it probably was just because it was my birthday, I figured. I saw a great short-sleeved raw silk shirt that was this icy silvery-blue color that even I could see looked really great with my eyes. It fit really nicely too. I'd started a regular gym routine again, and the cardio and free weights had really knocked off the extra few pounds and softness that had crept on when I was feeling the worst about things.

I shopped around a little more, but frankly it bored the shit out of me. After crossing off every item on my list, I was ready to head home. I hit the Hallmark store to get a nice card and wrapping paper for Robbie's gifts and headed home to shower and get ready to go out. I looked forward to it.

WHEN I got to Antonio's I went in like I usually did. I didn't see him. When I looked around, I heard the shower running. I yelled that I was there and went to sit in the den. There were computer parts everywhere, and the room was totally a fucking mess. He had half-assembled *somethings* in there that he had explained, when I was half listening, were workstations.

He was totally into the design work he started and created some really interesting shapes and curves that looked oddly graceful. I wished now that I'd paid more attention to what he told me about all of his ideas. Now that I'd the time to study them, I could see wanting one for my house.

I was running my hand up and over the beam that had small speakers imbedded in it when I heard him coming out of the bedroom. "These are terrific," I told him and turned around. And had to do one motherfucker of a double take and kind of hope he didn't notice my jaw was hanging open.

He'd traded in his loose 3XL shirts, baggy jeans, and Doc Martens for a pair of cream-colored slacks that hugged his ass and a pale green dress shirt that strained across his chest. And dress shoes. He looked fucking amazing. "Thanks," he said and grinned. Fuck, I must've said that out loud.

He looked me up and down and gave a wolf whistle. "Like that T-shirt, man, looks great with your eyes," he said and walked a circle around me. I felt a little hot and wondered if he'd cut the air conditioning back. "You about ready to go, baby?" he asked and patted my arm.

I followed him out to that big-ass truck and buckled in. We made small talk all the way over to the steakhouse, and it was nice. When we got there, we parked in the back corner of the lot so nobody could ding his baby. It was already dark, but this was a pretty good area of town so I wasn't worried.

The hostess had our reservation, and we were guided quickly to a very nice table. One of the servers came by and explained the whole concept of the place, and I liked that we could choose from all those meats, because Southern guys can eat some cow.

"What made you want to come here?" I asked. Not that I minded.

"It's your birthday," he explained, "and I wanted this evening to be something special." He reached over and squeezed my hand and then opened his napkin. I looked around and saw the place was very nicely decorated, dark wood beams and private tables scattered around the huge space. I noticed lots of couples, and we weren't the only two men together either.

Now, you don't get to be the chief financial officer and manage a five million dollar budget without having a minimum of two brain cells that fire off together. The pieces started to fall together, and I could feel my heart beat faster and my head spin.

Jason was staying with his mom even though it was Antonio's night to have him. Told me to dress pretty. Wore an outfit I would swear on a stack of Bibles wasn't in his closet last week. Brought me to a romantic restaurant.

"Antonio," I said and waited 'til he looked me in the eyes. "What's going on?" He looked at me and just smiled. "Are we on a… *date*?" His slow smile and the heat in his eyes were almost answer enough. I sat back in the chair to give myself a second to regroup and decide how to proceed. I finally got it—this was a game. Antonio was just fucking with me and trying to make me laugh. I just shrugged and deadpanned, "Okay. But I'm not putting out. Not for a steak dinner."

That lightened things up, and we both went to the buffet area and checked out the offerings. God, a man could die happy in a place like this. And damn if Antonio wasn't all up in my personal space. Reached up to say something low in my ear. Bumped shoulders.

I played the game right back. I turned back and put my mouth right against the shell of his ear and breathed an answer back. Once we were back at the table, I moved around behind him and guided him to his seat with my hand on the small of his back. Then let it slide down and cup his ass. I really enjoyed the shiver I saw and felt.

HetBoy might make the ladies quiver, but I was used to taking charge and being with a man. He wanted to see what a date with a guy felt like, bring it on.

I played it up. Moaned at how good the steaks were, although I really didn't have to pretend there. They were fucking amazing. Ordered wine and licked the rim. Sat back and ran my hand across my chest and down to my stomach and groaned about how full I was. And watched him notice the way the shirt hugged my chest when I pulled the fabric tight.

I thought he'd back off and realize he was playing a dangerous game. But every move I made ratcheted up the heat in his eyes. Even the blush I put on his face didn't stop him from looking. What I saw in those looks made me feel a little funny myself. My body was responding to the game. I could feel my nipples pebbling against the roughness of the shirt. My cock was starting to wake up from deep freeze.

"Would you gentlemen care for any dessert this evening?" the cute little Argentinean gaucho asked. He looked back and forth between us, and I caught his eyes on both of our crotches.

"No, babe, I think I'll take my dessert home now and eat it at my leisure," I drawled and hid a wince. God, I was cheesy but it got the reaction I wanted. Envy and wistfulness from the hot boy checking out my guy, and something like a choked growl from Antonio.

Don't fuck with the bear, I thought. You risk getting mauled. I never once thought Antonio was going to cash any of the checks his ass was writing. He would come to his senses and remember he liked women, then we'd go back to being best buddies.

That worked until we got to the truck, where I found myself shoved against the door and I was the one that got mauled. He held me there while his mouth attacked mine, and there wasn't a bit of gentleness in the kiss. It was rough and raw and tasted like hunger and lust and steak. It brought all my bottled-up need to take control out. Before he knew what happened, I slammed his ass around, turning the tables on him and taking control of the kiss. Reaching behind him, I grabbed him by the neck to hold his mouth on mine and put my other hand on his dick.

I could feel his groan when I squeezed. I swallowed it and gave his cock a few rough strokes and felt him tense up. His hands grabbed air, and I vaguely registered he didn't know what to do with them, if it was okay to touch me. He choked out a long, sexy moan, and I felt the warm stickiness through his pants. He sagged against me, panting. I held him up until he shook it off and got himself back under control.

When he pulled me into a hug, I heard what sounded like, "I love you," breathed into my neck.

"Are you okay now?" I asked while rubbing circles on his back and holding him.

He nodded and raised his head. "Are you?"

I laughed a little and smacked his ass. "Peachy. I haven't done that since, ummm, Tommy Weatherly in high school." I thought, *what the hell*, then reached over, took his keys out of his front pocket, and hit the lock release.

"Get your ass in and let's get back to your place. I think you need a shower and some sweats." I chuckled. He opened the door and climbed in the passenger seat without an argument.

Oddly, the quiet drive back home was comfortable and relaxed. I kept waiting for him to freak out and start the whole *I'm not gay* thing. Waited for his anger, accusations, a fight. Something. Not this... familiarity.

We got there and went in, and he headed to the bedroom to take a shower. "Come in and keep me company," he said and stripped off his sticky pants. *Why not*, I thought, and went in and sat on the bed. He started the shower and climbed in. "Get comfortable," he stuck his head out and said. I kicked off my shoes and socks and flopped down on the bed and started to wonder what we were doing and yelled out to him, "What are we doing?"

"Mark, don't fucking get in your head about this. It's your birthday, we had a good time. A nice date. 'Cause yeah, that's what it was. And you're gonna spend the night and get some sleep and we can talk about it tomorrow. Okay?"

Actually that sounded pretty fucking good. So I stripped down to my boxer briefs and slid under the covers. The sound of the water was soothing, and before I knew it I was asleep.

I WOKE up sometime later during the night and was on my side, pressed into Antonio's back. The debate over whether to get up, get dressed, and go home versus staying in bed and not moving took all of about ten seconds. The next time I opened my eyes, I was alone in the bed and the sun was up. I stretched and scratched. The need to piss was greater than the temptation to just lie there.

When I was finished, I decided to brush my teeth and shower. He kept the bathroom stocked with extra toiletries. I grabbed a pair of his sweats and went into the kitchen and called his name. "In here," he yelled from the den, "grab you some coffee and come on in."

He was doing something with the computer parts strewed across the table. I grabbed my cup of coffee and pulled a chair over so I could see what he was up to. "Making any progress?" I tried, since I couldn't tell what the hell he was doing.

"Yeah, I'm taking everything apart and putting all the pieces back together in a new way and hoping I didn't fuck anything up." He cut his eyes toward me.

Guess that was my cue. "Nothing's broken," I said and reached over to touch his back. "But I think we need to talk, don't you?" He nodded and I motioned with my head for him to join me over on the couch. He grabbed his mug and we sat down, not right against each other but not on opposite sides either.

"So, last night," I prompted to get the conversation started. He started this dance, and I needed him to explain the steps. He shrugged the tiniest bit and started talking, staring into his mug.

"It was your birthday and I wanted it to be special. I wanted it to be with *me*." He looked up at me. "Don't know what the fuck I'm doing here, but a date's a good place to start." The smile in his eyes matched the one on his face.

"But," and I kind of stalled out there. I thought he was playing, making the date a game, entertainment. "But, fucking help me out here. Start *what*, exactly? I don't understand," I admitted. *What was he looking for?* I wondered. I was afraid he didn't know either.

His next words confirmed it. "Man, I don't *know*! I want to be with you, be *with* you. I've never done this before, Mark. Not with my ex-wife even." And I knew it was true. He'd told me how he only had married her because she was pregnant with Jason. He never was in love with her. Never really *wanted* to be with her. "I've never been in love before, not with her, with any woman, and sure as hell not with a man."

"Are you saying—" He jerked his gaze to me and nodded, looking fucking miserable.

"I don't know what to do here, man. Look, can I tell you something and you promise me you won't fucking get pissed or leave or some shit?" he asked. I thought about it. How bad it could be? But I slowly nodded.

He took a deep breath and plunged in. "I love you and I'm pretty sure I'm *in* love with you and have been for a while. For years. I know I'm not the kind of guy for a man like you. I'm not successful and I can barely keep all my bills paid, and you, man, you are so together and can have any guy you want. You deserve a guy who can be all that back for you, and here I am not knowing what the hell I'm doing. It scares the fuck out of me because of Jason and what if his mom finds out and tries to keep him away from me. I—" He looked away from me.

I took over and filled the rest of it in for him. "You aren't gay. And you don't want to be."

Still with his head down, he reached over to grab my arm, and I guess he was afraid I'd leave after that was out in the open. I thought about it. I had too much self-respect and too many years of being out to hide in the closet for anybody. If I were to look closely inside, I wasn't sure what it was I felt for Antonio. Love, yes. Respect and gratitude. And yes, I was attracted physically. Fuck, who wouldn't be?

It was only fair that I was honest with him. "I don't know if I'm ready to be *anything* with you, Antonio. I like you a lot, and yeah, I love you. But I won't be your dirty little secret either. Maybe you should take some time and think about it all." I moved to get up but he pulled me back down right next to him.

He grabbed me and kissed me again, a little desperately. "All I've done is think about this. About you. Since before Brian died."

I tensed up.

"I'd have never done anything then. Fuck, I can barely believe I'm saying it now." He kissed me again. I still couldn't say anything, but I kissed him back. "Please, Mark, baby, please," he crooned in between kisses, "please give me a chance. Tell me what to do." And I'm not sure whether it was the *please* or the taste of his submission, but I was rock-hard.

I took control then, of the situation, the kiss, Antonio. I looked him in the eye and asked, "Do you trust me?" He nodded and leaned back in for another kiss. I gave it to him, then pushed him a little away, so I could move, raised my hips and shed the sweats. My hard cock bounced up, and he looked at it, then into my eyes. I reached out and brought his hand to it, wrapping it around my shaft then closed my hand over his.

I asked again, "Do you trust me?" He nodded again, and I pulled his head in for another kiss, then pushed it toward my cock. He looked up questioningly, and I said, "Suck me."

I needed to know. Know if he could do this with me. It's one thing for a straight guy to get head or fuck another man. That doesn't make him gay. But to be the passive partner, to suck, get fucked, that would tell me what I needed to know.

He looked for just a minute, then opened his mouth and closed it on the head. I guided his hand to keep stroking and held his face between my hands. Then I slowly pumped into his mouth. I didn't want his first time to make him gag and ruin it for him.

He started to moan and that made my hips buck. When he didn't gag, I thrust a little deeper. His other hand was in his own sweats, jacking hard and fast. The tingle and slow burn of orgasm started in my balls. His grunts and moans made my dick twitch, and I knew it would be a matter of seconds. I started to pull away, but he sucked harder, refusing to let go, so I went with it. When I started to shoot, he swallowed, and I felt him start to jerk when he came hard.

I yanked him up into a kiss, and tasted myself in his mouth. He looked dazed but satisfied. I pulled him beside me, into my arms and cradled him as I laid us both down on the couch. "We can try this. I won't put any pressure on you, but make me a promise," I whispered to him.

"What?" he rasped out.

"Don't fucking leave me. Don't break my heart." And I couldn't look at him. He nodded into my chest, closed his eyes, and smiled.

CHAPTER EIGHTEEN

September 2006

THE weather in San Francisco was fantastic any time of year, but the sun seemed to be out every day I had been there, and I was so relaxed I thought I was turning into Jell-O.

It didn't hurt that my friends Bill and Chris had wined and dined me all over Marin and Sausalito. I'd long ago done all the touristy shit, and Castro Street left me a little high and dry. For some it was the Mecca of gay life, but for me it seemed a little… redundant. If I was looking to get laid, I'd have headed there in a heartbeat, but that wasn't why I was there.

Antonio was due to drive up from Los Angeles later. He'd decided on the spur of the moment to visit his mom and let her see Jason for the first time in several years. His sister also lived in the area, so it made sense to do it before school started. It was a little funny that this trip came up so suddenly when he found out I was going to be out there. Alone. In San Francisco. With a million other gay guys.

And the phone call was, I don't know, hysterical. Ridiculous. Fucking amazing. "I decided to come out and visit my mom and sister. When can I see you?"

I waited while what he said sunk in. "What the fuck, Antonio? I've been here twelve hours."

"You don't want to see me?" he carefully asked.

Fuck. Fuckity fuck. "When will you be here?"

He needed to leave again early the next morning to get back to L.A. and his mom and Jason. She wasn't in the best of health, it turned out, and he didn't want to leave Jason with her very long. Antonio was also hoping to visit some of the suppliers of computer components he used, to talk to them about some design ideas. He really should have stayed in Los Angeles but had insisted on coming up for the day. And night. It was beyond cute that he insisted on seeing me. I couldn't help but laugh and tell him no way was he pissing on my leg to mark his territory.

Hanging up on his sputtering denial, I'd arranged for us to take a tour of the wine country. I was up and ready when he called me from his rental and let me know he was downstairs. I grabbed my wallet and key and went down to the front of the hotel. I climbed in and said hi, then started to give him directions. Before I knew it I was pulled into a kiss. "Now that's a proper welcome," he said and laughed.

We headed across the Golden Gate Bridge and up into Marin. The conversation was light and fun, and it wasn't long before we pulled into the first winery. We got out and walked around until the tour started. Afterward, they always gave customers the opportunity to buy a bottle of their wine and light snacks, so I grabbed a bottle of a Shiraz, some cheese, and baguettes.

We walked out into the vineyard and sat and drank wine and fed each other cheese on crusty French bread. I asked him about the flight, and how Jason was doing. How his mother and sister were. "I love them and it's good to see them. Jason needs to know his family on my side so he sees where he comes from," he said.

The sun was warm and nice, so we stretched out on our backs, talked about nothing, and dozed. I woke to him leaning over me. He studied my face and eyes for a long moment, then whispered, "I missed you" and kissed me. This one was tender and spoke of things I wasn't really ready to talk about right now. My heart gave a little leap, but I pushed it back down.

Antonio was fine with showing how much he cared for me, loved me, when we were alone, or in a safe place where nobody knew us. But he was still scared of Jason finding out we were anything other than buddies and the news getting back to his ex-wife. The fact that he had an ironclad custody agreement didn't mean anything to him. He almost lost his son once and that seemed to make everything else secondary.

And could I really blame him? I didn't have a kid, but I was an uncle and would kill anyone who tried to mess with my little nieces and nephews. I just didn't get that our relationship was a danger. Jason already knew me and was comfortable with me. The ex had met me, and I'd even picked him up and dropped him off a couple of times when last-minute massage clients came up.

Right now, that wasn't a deal breaker. We were just starting whatever this was, and it was nice. Since my birthday, we had a couple of sleepovers. There was a solid connection based on friendship, and the sex, the sex was great. We'd exchanged blowjobs and jacked off together but hadn't taken it further yet.

I wasn't sure I was ready to commit to anybody right now. Much less a man with the issues Antonio had. But that didn't stop me from taking what was offered. The sweet kisses. The promise of more.

"It's about time for us to head back to the hotel so we can beat the traffic across the bridge," I told him. He grunted and laid his head on my chest. I pulled him into a hug and held him for a few minutes, then popped his ass and told him to get moving.

"Fucker," he laughed as he climbed off me and up.

"If you're a very good boy the rest of the afternoon, we'll see," I growled. He stood over me for a second, just looking at me until he got what I meant. The slow, red flush that went over his face told me everything. He reached down to help me up and we made our way to the car and headed back to the city.

WE WENT out to dinner at the oldest Italian restaurant in the city. It'd been rebuilt after the two big earthquakes in 1906 and 1989 that made San Francisco such an interesting place to live. The meal was terrific and relaxed. But Antonio looked at me and blushed more than once.

Finally I asked him what was going on. "What you said earlier," he leaned over and whispered to me.

I thought back and then remembered what he was talking about. "So you mean you like the idea of me fucking you?"

He looked everywhere but at me and said, "Jesus, do you have to announce it to the world?"

I grinned and said, "Waiting for the answer, babe."

He nodded and fiddled with his flatware.

"I think that can be arranged. Want dessert? They have great *panna cotta* here." I was playing it cool but inside, I was anything but. It felt like all the blood in my body was pooled in my crotch and that was at war with where I needed it to be able to think. Because taking this step meant something to me. It took things from just messing around to baring my soul. I couldn't just fuck—I wasn't built that way. I made love.

In the cab on the way back to the hotel, I asked the driver to stop at a drugstore. He caught my eye in the rearview mirror and grinned. I winked and reached over and rubbed Antonio's leg. He started to pull away, but then relaxed. I leaned over and said, "Nobody knows us here, it's okay." He nodded. After I ran in and bought condoms and lube, we arrived back at the hotel and went upstairs.

He'd brought his overnight bag in with him earlier and looked ready to grab it and hit the shower. I pulled him into a hug and kiss first, then felt him relax.

"We need to talk about this first," I said. I wanted him to be comfortable, but I needed him to know what this step meant to me too. There was a small loveseat in the room, and we sat facing each other, legs tangled up.

I took a deep breath and dove right in. "I haven't been with anyone except Brian, well, and now you, in over ten years." I stopped to let it sink in and tried to find the right words to explain how I felt. He nodded for me to go on, and I told him the whole story of how Brian and I'd met. How we became friends and were for several years. Then how the friendship turned into love. When I realized I loved him I wasn't with anyone until he and I decided we wanted to be together.

"When he cheated on me, it almost destroyed me. Antonio," I started, and all the emotions that were my relationship with Brian were right there, right then. "I loved him, I trusted him. We said 'I love you' and 'There won't be anybody else,' and then he did that to me." I could feel the tears threaten to drop.

He started to reach out for me, but I put out a hand. I needed to get through this alone. "And I found a way to forgive him, but there wasn't anybody else when he was gone."

I reached up to rub my eyes and looked at him. "What I'm trying to say is, I can't do casual, and that's what we've been doing. We're buddies, and now we have benefits. But, Antonio, if we do this... if we... if I make love to you, I mean it." I reached out to him then and grabbed his hand. Squeezed tight and saw the vulnerability in his eyes.

"And it has to mean that *you* mean it too. That you want to be mine. That we're going somewhere with this," I said. I pulled his hand to my chest. "If you don't mean it, I'm done. I won't be giving anyone another chance."

I stopped there. I'd probably said too much already, put too much on him. Asked more than he could, or would, give. So then I waited.

"Can I talk now?" he asked. I nodded. He kept his hand over my heart and bent down to kiss where his hand lay. "I never meant for this to happen. I never pictured myself in love, didn't know I was capable of it. Fuck, the only person that ever got that far in was my buddy Jake."

He caught what sounded like a sob in his throat before it could escape. "We grew up together, and when I got out of school, right before I went to boot camp, Jake got into a thing with a gang in the hood. I, he... fuck Mark, they shot him before I could get there and he died in my arms. On the goddamned street. And I loved him. Fuck, maybe I was in love with him, I don't know." He shook his head and looked away to compose himself.

I held onto that hand on my chest. When he got himself back under control, he started again. "I can't promise you it'll be easy for me. That I won't be fucking scared off my ass. But I know this much." And he pushed me backward and climbed on top of me. "I love you, and I will do anything, *everything*, to be the man you deserve. Don't give up on me. Please. I'll beg you if you want me to, but please Mark, just don't give up on me."

There aren't many moments in life when someone bares his heart and soul wide open for you. I was lucky, I was blessed with it twice. Brian, now Antonio.

"I won't, but you have to promise you won't either," I said.

He reached down and held my head between his two strong hands. "I won't. I swear it to you," he breathed. "Make love to me, Mark. Make me yours."

I nodded. He kissed my forehead and stared at me for a minute, then got up. Took his bag and went to the bathroom and started the shower.

I laid there for a couple of minutes and said a couple of prayers. Thanked God for letting me find someone again. Whispered to Brian that I would always love and remember him, and that he was right when he said Antonio loved me. Then I got up to get myself ready, get my iPod out and lower the light. Opened the condom package and lube and set them on the nightstand.

When Antonio was finished showering, I was already waiting to jump in and freshen up. I gave him a quick hug from behind as he stood in front of the mirror brushing his teeth. Let him feel me against his back, ran my hands down his front and cupped him. Ground my half-hard cock against his rock-hard ass, then jumped in the shower. "Wait for me in bed," I told him.

When I was finished, I could hear Tuck and Patty on my iPod in the other room. The lights were just bright enough that I could see him stretched out waiting for me.

I went to the bed and lay on my side. He rolled over to face me. I pulled him to me and kissed him. I started it slow and easy, wanting him to see how much I cared. I let him explore me with his hands. I ran mine down his back and grabbed his ass, stroked and squeezed it.

When the kiss started to gain in intensity and heat, I moved on top of him and deepened it. His mouth was on fire. He sucked my tongue like he had my cock. I could feel how hard he was, and how he ground his hips up against mine to get some friction. He still shaved his crotch, and my dick appreciated the smoothness and the hardness.

Being with him was different, because he was used to being the aggressor, I could tell. I worked to tame him, make him remember what being relaxed and letting me take the lead felt like. His body knew what it wanted, and I knew how to make him feel good.

I slowly pulled away from the kiss to move my attention to his jaw, lightly dropping kisses behind his ear and nibbling his earlobe. He tasted like salt as I let my tongue trail down his neck to his shoulder. My hands roamed over his chest and down his sides, stroking him like I did during a massage, long and slow and steady. My mouth painted long wet stripes across his chest and lingered around his nipples.

I heard him as he murmured, "Please," and I let him have what he wanted. I sucked and licked and bit his nipples, worked one with my mouth and the other with my fingers. Antonio thrust his chest up begging, sometimes for me to stop and sometimes to never stop. Always *More, please.* I had him totally into the feelings, the heat.

When I raked the flat of my tongue and scraped my teeth over his stomach and abs to his crotch, he groaned, and I moved between his legs, forced his legs wider. My mouth sucked the crease where his leg joined groin, and I raked my teeth across that thin, tender flesh. He shivered, his cock leaked drops onto his belly.

I sucked in one of his balls and rolled it around, then moved my hands under him to cup his ass. I firmly massaged both cheeks, spreading them wide. I let him escape my mouth then took both of his balls in and tugged them with my teeth. Antonio's head rolled from side to side. His hands clenched into the sheets. He alternated between looking down to see me and clenching his eyes shut against the pleasure I was giving him.

His cock demanded attention, so I let his balls go and focused my attention on the shaft and the large vein that ran up the bottom. When I reached the head and swirled my tongue on the underside, he yelled out, begging, "Suck me, for God's sake." I plunged my head down, and he slid all the way to the back of my throat. He yelled my name when I stretched his ass cheeks open and worked my thumbs toward the hole. I massaged around the tight little pucker while I bobbed up and down on him, taking it in on every stroke.

After a minute or two of sucking, I pulled off his shaft and licked back down to his balls, then used my shoulders to lift his thighs, opening his hole. When I moved my tongue from his testicles and licked his perineum. His ass clenched, the tension built back in his body. "Shhh," I gentled, "I have this, trust me." He laid his head back and relaxed a little. I blew light breaths against his pucker to watch it tighten. My tongue flat, I licked right over the opening.

He gasped and I did it again. His breathing was ragged and fast. I blew another light warm blast of air on it and asked, "Nobody's ever rimmed you before?"

He groaned out, "*No*," and I licked across the bud again. Then made my tongue into a point and speared hard and fast right on the hole.

I was surprised the people in the room next door didn't hear his moan. Bingo. I darted my tongue against his opening, teasing it up more and more. I nibbled and lightly bit at it. He sucked in a ragged breath. I spread his ass wide, and thrust my tongue in as deep as I could. I felt him reach for his cock and warned him, "Don't touch it or I'll stop."

"Please, Mark. I need something more. You're driving me fucking crazy. Fuck me, man. Holy shit, I had no idea. I want to feel you in me. Now." He rolled his head back and forth on the pillow.

"I'll take care of you, Antonio." I reached over to the nightstand and grabbed the supplies. I tore the condom open first before I opened the lube. They were a bitch to open with slippery hands and always used to rip the package *and* the rubber when I tried with my teeth. After

I rolled it on, I took the top off the lube and leaned back down to lick and tongue him again.

This time, I slicked up a finger and started working it in beside my tongue. I got it almost in and raked my teeth up his shaft again. I knew the head was too sensitive and he would shoot too soon. I wanted to be in him when he came.

He took the finger with no problem. My mouth distracted him as I worked another finger in. I moved them around, fucked in and out. His muscles relaxed and took me. I sought out his prostate, and when I hit it with both fingers he almost came up off the bed. I reached up and rubbed his stomach with one hand while massaging that little bundle of nerves inside. He was as ready as I could make him.

And my patience was beginning to wear thin. My cock was harder than it'd been in a long time. I wanted in.

I pulled my fingers out and moved up between his thighs, pushing his knees toward his chest. I looked him in the eyes and let him know I was ready. "Are you ready now?" I asked. His blown pupils told me he was there, and he could only nod.

"It might be more comfortable your first time on your hands and knees, but I have to see you," I said and kissed him. "Kiss you." I licked my tongue across his lips again.

I reached down and positioned the head against his hole and pushed in. There was a little resistance, and he grunted. I held still and leaned in to take his mouth with mine. One hand worked down to stroke his cock, and the other snaked behind his head to hold him against my mouth. I eased in further and sucked his tongue, and took what I needed. What he gave me.

As I stroked his cock, I started to move inside him. When I was all the way in, I pulled off his mouth and asked, "You okay?"

Antonio reached both hands to my shoulders and pulled me against him. "Make love to me, Mark. Make me yours."

It was like a bell sounded, like a gun went off. I pounded into him and attacked his mouth with mine. His legs were on my shoulders, and

I fucked him hard and fast, tilted him until I found the right angle and hit his prostate again. He yelled into my mouth and I kept it up, hit it with every stroke or two until I felt his cock begin to swell and his hole to tighten.

"Come for me, Antonio. Want you coming around my cock," I panted into his ear. I felt it when he began to shoot, and the tightness drove me faster toward my own finish. When the waves of tingling down my spine to my balls reached their peak, I bit down on his neck and shot into his ass. I lost my rhythm and pounded in, deeper and deeper until I was spent.

When I let his legs slip off my shoulders and pulled out of him, he flopped bonelessly, sweaty with me half on top of him. I kissed him, lightly and with love. His eyes were closed and his lips were swollen, and his breathing slowly evened out. "You with me there, baby?" I asked.

He opened his eyes and looked at me. "Now I'm yours."

I kissed him and whispered, "Yeah. Mine."

CHAPTER NINETEEN

December 2006

"ARE you ready to go?" I yelled. Antonio was still in his bedroom and we had to go pick up Jason. I already had things loaded in the truck and didn't want to be too late to Dad's house. This was the first family function we were going to *together*. Even if nobody knew it. I went in and he was sitting on the edge of the bed. I plopped down next to him and bumped shoulders. "Talk to me."

He let out a deep sigh. "I'm not sure I can do this."

Well, I'd expected this sooner or later. Thanksgiving was easier. It was just two friends, and he spent most of the time out in the work shed with Dad and Robbie, talking about how he could do the welding for the entertainment unit the two were building for the family room. My offer of help was politely declined by all three. I'd retreated to the kitchen, secretly grateful but outwardly cursing their macho craftsman bullshit to anybody who would listen.

This was different and I planned to hit it head-on. "So, what is it? You think I'm going to bend you over the table and show them we're together? Or is it Jason? You've gotta help me out some here." I waited.

He put a hand on my thigh and said, "I haven't ever had somebody I can call my own before and... and accept me and my boy and make us all a family. When I was with Jeanine, her parents did everything and they treated me like something they scraped off the bottom of their fucking shoes."

He needed to get this out and I let him. "I like your family. They're so cool. I never had this." He'd felt surer and opened up a little bit at a time when he got back from California. His mother drank, favored his sister and when his dad died she let him run the streets. It was a miracle he decided to join the army and didn't end up like Jake, just a regret. A memory.

"Antonio, they love you. They know you helped me after Brian died, know you found Robbie. For that alone, you're fucking golden. It's there for you. All you have to do is reach out for it, man," I told him. They wanted me to be happy. And shit, I hadn't told him half of them already figured out about us.

Patty and Jennifer cornered me after dinner at Thanksgiving and wanted to know when, not if, I had *taken his flower*. I choked and told them they'd been reading too much gay romance shit. If they knew, Ray and Robert knew. Robbie gave me a look too, and I stared his little punk ass down. But he was whispering to Dad and I didn't dare ask about what.

And I was holding on to a secret I couldn't tell Antonio yet.

"Your choice, man. I hope you'll make the right one. I need to go though. You coming?" I stood and held out my hand. He shook his head but grabbed my wrist, and I yanked him up against me. He deserved a kiss for that. The one I gave him was hot and dirty, and left him a little wrinkled and dazed by the time we got in the truck.

JASON was ready to go when we got to Jeanine's house and had a shopping bag with a couple of things in it that he quickly stowed in the back of the truck. He wouldn't tell his dad what he had, but he snuck me a grin.

Jesus, he looked so much like Antonio these days. He was fourteen, almost fifteen now, and had a girlfriend at school. He and Robbie spent a lot of time on the phone. Now that Robbie could drive, they hung out together too. But Antonio was a fucking ostrich with his head in the sand.

"So what'd you get? Lots of coal and switches?" I joked with him.

"Eww, sounds more like something you would get. Switches and other stuff," he threw back at me. I almost spewed Coke all over the truck. That little shit. I snuck a glance at Antonio but he missed it, or chose to ignore it. The brat ignored my glare and went on to tell me about his new PlayStation 3 and all the new games he could play online with his friends.

When we pulled into Dad's driveway, I saw Robbie and some older guy in a heated discussion out on the street. The guy gripped Robbie by the arm and was trying to get him inside the car. Oh *fuck* no! But before I could get there, Antonio already had the piece of garbage by the neck and made him let Robbie go. I sent Jason into the house to get Dad and ran over to where he bounced the guy's head against the car window.

"I told you to leave him alone, you fucker. How the hell did you find him here?" Antonio was growling. My heart pounded as I put it all together. This was Zev. I knew it. I grabbed Antonio's arm and pulled him off the guy. Zev looked dazed and there was blood running down from what looked like a broken nose. I could see Dad coming out of the house with his gun. Shit.

"Antonio, you take Robbie and go over and show Dad he's okay and calm Jason down," I said. When he hesitated, I pushed him and ordered, "*Now.*"

Once he was out of hearing range I got up in the man's face and asked, "Are you Zev?" When he nodded, I grabbed him by the front of the shirt and pulled him in really close. "You listen close, 'cause I ain't saying this but once. That boy is *my* family now. He's got a home, he's got people that love him. And don't think we don't know how to fuckin' hide a body when we need to."

His eyes got huge and he started to sputter. I shook him good and pulled him in right against my face. "My daddy, that guy there with the gun? He'll shoot you if you show your face in this area again. If Robbie comes home with so much as a hair out of place, we know how to find you. And just so you know, Robbie told me everything." I shook him to emphasize it. "Every-fucking-thing. I go to the cops, you won't get out of jail. And you know what they do to chickenhawks like you in jail?"

He just glared.

I let him go and straightened my jacket. "We understand each other here?" I asked. He nodded. "No, fucker, say it. We understand each other?"

He pulled what little dignity he had left around him. He shoved me hard against the chest and I stumbled back. "Yeah. We understand each other. He's not worth it. Guess he's kinda worn out now anyway," he snarled, looked at Antonio and Dad comforting Robbie. Then back at me.

I looked at him and tried to imagine what, how, such filth came to be. I just shook my head. I was done. "You have 'til I get back over there and then all bets are off, Zev. If you're still here, I'll personally get Dad's shotgun and blow your fuckin' nuts off. You've got about twenty seconds." I walked off feeling so disgusted that I might've actually followed through with it. I heard the car door slam and the sound of tires squealing as he tore off. My hillbilly act worked.

Robbie was in tears and huddled up against Dad and Jason, but when he saw me coming back over, he ran straight to me and hugged me so tight I had trouble breathing. I petted him and whispered to him to calm down while Antonio and Dad hovered. When he got back under control, I looked over to Dad. "You know who that was?" I asked, and he nodded. He gripped his gun tighter. "He won't be back. I made it clear I knew some things he doesn't want out there. We won't be seeing him again." And I had plans for that fucker. *Just wait, you scumbag.*

Robbie transferred his hug of death over to Dad, and I couldn't help but smile at the bond those two had. I looked up and Antonio was tensed up. "What's wrong?"

He looked at me hard for a couple of seconds then I was crushed against him, and he was kissing me. "Don't you fucking dare put yourself in danger like that. I can't lose you. Fuck. I love you. Promise me," he got out between kisses.

"I promise, Antonio. I love you too. But, um, Jason…," I said, and he froze, then dropped his head against my shoulder and sighed. I held him and whispered in his ear that everything would be okay. I caught Jason's eye and he came over.

He wrapped his arms around his father from behind. "Dad, it's okay. I was worried about you and Mark too. I'm glad Mr. Jennings had his gun." We stayed like that for a minute, then he went on. "Dad," he said very gently "I know about you and Mark."

At that, Antonio looked up at me with startled eyes. I just looked and nodded. He pulled back and Jason let him go, but sidled up to him in a side hug. He was already almost as tall as his dad, just not as filled out. He was trying to grow a moustache and it was about five hairs, but he was so proud of it and his newly deep voice.

"I've known how you felt about him for a long time. I really like Mark, and don't be mad at him, but I asked him last week when he took me Christmas shopping if you two were together."

Antonio just looked back and forth between us, face showing shock and then anger, then what I recognized as resolve. "Oh he did, huh?" he said and glared at me. "And don't think you and me won't be talking about this later."

He turned to Jason. "What do you think about it?" I already knew, but he needed to hear it from his son.

Jason squeezed Antonio's shoulder and said, "I think it's awesome. I have three daddies," he giggled. "Who else can say that? And that means I get hella presents, right? Wait 'til you see what I got you two." Antonio bumped heads with him and pulled him into a real hug. "Seriously, Dad. I love you. And I love Mark. If you two are happy together, I think it's pretty fucking great."

Antonio swatted his butt and said, "Language, boy. You ain't too big for a spanking."

"I bet that's what Mark says to you, too." He laughed as he escaped from his dad and ran behind me for protection, like he'd done for all these years when he and Antonio played. "Just don't let me catch you doing it," he cackled. I couldn't help but laugh. But I also saw the concern in Antonio's eyes. I looked around and everyone else had gone back into the house to give us some privacy.

"Jason, you better tell him the rest so he can deal with it now," I told the boy. Antonio jerked around to look at me. "Just listen to him," I said. He nodded and the three of us sat at the picnic table Dad kept in the front yard.

"Mom knows too," he said bluntly. Antonio got really pale. I knew it was his worst fear. "Dad, she doesn't care. She said that explains why it didn't work with you and her. She has Gary now and they love each other." He looked at me, and then his father. "And you love Mark, don't you?"

There was silence and I feared for one second, one long fucking second that he would deny it. Deny me. Just play it off as a misunderstanding. Then he reached across the table and took my hand. "More than anything, son. I know it's gotta be weird, because it is for me too. But I love Mark. I don't know if that makes me gay but I love him so much."

And I could breathe again. Goddamn it but there must be some dust blowing around out here, because my eyes got all watery. I had to wipe them.

"If you marry him, then which one of you has to wear the dress?" the little smart-ass said. A beat of silence, and we looked at each other.

Antonio blushed red, and I turned to his son and said, evilly, "You, flower girl." Damn if the blushing wasn't a family trait.

"All right, let's go in. I'm sure my sisters are gonna *love* this. Get ready for the Patty and Jennifer show," I warned. We all got up and grabbed bags and boxes out of the truck and made our way inside.

IT COULD'VE been worse, I guess. Patty and Jennifer were waiting about five feet inside the door with arms crossed, feet tapping. Antonio and I exchanged glances. I shrugged, looked the wenches right in the eye and said, "Mine. All mine. You can look but don't touch. Got a problem with that?" I walked by and into the living room.

I heard Antonio behind me. "His. What he said." They laughed, hugged him and Jason, and I could hear his protests all the way in the other room.

I didn't catch too much shit from the rest of the family, either. Brenda and Linda, the God Squad, pretty much ignored us. The wound with Bren was still too fresh for me to say anything without a blowup, and it was Christmas. Linda I ignored as usual. Jennifer had Robert whipped, and he wouldn't care.

Sam surprised me.

"You sure about this one?" he asked me. I looked at him and tried to figure what to say, mentally prepping myself for the hatred and snide remarks.

"Yeah, I'm sure," I said. Fuck it, I thought. Nothing he could say could hurt me anymore. Not now.

He nodded and said, "Good. I don't understand it, but it's not my place to. Just, be happy little brother. You deserve it." He awkwardly reached out and gave me a hug. Patted my shoulders hard and moved off.

I stood there a minute and couldn't decide whether to laugh or cry. Antonio came in then and I grabbed him, ducked into the bathroom and locked the door.

I slammed him against it and kissed him hard and rough. He froze, then gave back as good as he got. He pulled back and said, "Fuck, what's got you worked up? Whatever it is, I like it."

I reached down, unsnapped his jeans, pushed them around his thighs, and dropped to my knees. He was going commando so that made it even easier for what I wanted. "Mark, what the—" He moaned when I took him in my mouth.

My tongue swirled around the head and crown, and I rubbed the flat of it against that little spot right under the slit. He hardened quickly and I swallowed him whole. I reached around and grabbed his ass, pulling him into my throat as deeply as I could get him. The man couldn't keep quiet when his cock was getting attention, so I pulled off and told him to grab a towel off the vanity. He did and shoved it against his mouth. I went back to his dick and took it in.

He took the hint, got into it. His hips began to pump that long cock in and out of my throat. I sucked him hard, wanting him to take pleasure and explode for me. I held my head still and let him fuck my mouth while I squeezed his ass and kneaded his hard cheeks to encourage him. He started to thrust harder and when his rhythm began to falter, I stroked a finger right over his pucker.

That got the result I wanted. He bucked hard. I worked in one finger and curled it onto his prostate. He pressed the towel hard against his mouth, but it wasn't enough to fully cover the shout he gave when he started shooting. I sucked hard and swallowed everything he gave me. When he started to soften, I licked him one last time and stood up, pulled his jeans back up and tucked and zipped him back in his pants.

I took the towel out of his mouth and replaced it with my lips. I let him taste us, his load and my desire, and he lazily kissed me back. His eyes were closed, and he looked totally blissed-out. When I let his mouth go, he smiled. "What did I do to deserve that?" I didn't say anything until he opened his eyes and looked at me.

"You love me," I said.

"Yeah, Mark, I do." His voice was soft and tender. "You know I do."

"Now I know how much. You didn't deny it."

He stared at me for a long moment. "I told you before I was scared. I still am. But, man, I realized something today." He launched off the door and crushed himself against me. "When I saw that fucker Zev put his hands on you, I wanted to hurt him. Bad." He breathed hard and was panting. "If anything happened to you, I needed you to know I'm him. I'm that guy."

I wasn't sure what he meant. "What guy, babe?"

He pulled back and looked at me with such tenderness in his eyes. "The guy who would do anything to deserve a man like you."

Fuck. I didn't want to lose my shit here. I wanted him home in my bed, where I could make love to him and force him to scream my name. Soon, I promised myself. Soon.

"You are, Antonio. You are that guy. And I'm that guy for you too.

OF COURSE Patty was standing outside the door when we cleaned up and went out. She opened her mouth to say something, but whatever it was died in her mouth. She looked at me, then Antonio, and what she saw there made her shut it. With love in her eyes she pulled us into a hug and held us for a long moment.

She cleared her throat and let us go. "Supper's ready, boys. Come on in and let Brenda say grace and let's eat.

Dinner was delicious. As always there was way too much to eat and not enough room to put it all. I made my way with a full plate to the cool table, and made sure Antonio had a place there too. Jason sat with Robbie at the kids' table and the two of them looked thick as thieves. The looks between them, huh. I glanced at Antonio and he just shrugged and smiled. Yeah, I guess whatever they were up to could wait.

It was the usual suspects at the cool table this year. Patty and Ray, Robert and Jennifer, me and Antonio. None of the others made a move to sit with us and that was fine too. Dad looked over at us and smiled. I was amazed at how relaxed and happy he looked this year. Having Robbie living there made him feel needed, I thought, since all of us were grown.

Robbie was prospering. He'd filled in and grown up, and was a little taller than me now. He had a family now, and I'd be taking him the next day to see his sister. Life for him was good.

I looked at Mom's chair, sitting empty. We still decorated it with garlands and lights every Christmas since Brian and I did it the first year she died. I thought how much she would've loved Robbie and wondered what she would make of Antonio. I closed my eyes for a minute and sent a quick prayer to her wherever she was, wished her peace and love, and hoped she was watching over her family tonight.

I felt a soft kiss against the back of my neck and opened my eyes, expecting that it was Antonio. He sat across from me taking to Ray, and when I turned around there was no one there.

I love you too, Mom.

CHAPTER TWENTY

September 2007

IT WAS raining by the time I got to Antonio's apartment. The day had been long and I was ready to have dinner, some wine, and relax with my guy. Any time auditors were in, my workload increased by a factor of ten. It always seemed like I was herding kittens when my attention needed to be focused on being professional and coherent. Not much fucking luck there.

So when I walked in I didn't expect to see boxes everywhere. Antonio had been working hard on his new designs for computer cabinetry and workstations. The walls were covered with drawings and every surface of his place had computer parts, welded components, and other stuff I was afraid to disturb. But not today. Most of that stuff was in boxes, and I could hear him in his bedroom making noise. I called out and walked in to see what was going on.

I stood there stunned for a minute and just looked over the scene in front of me. Antonio had everything he owned out of the closets and drawers and was packing it in suitcases and boxes. His clothes, everything. I could see it all but it just didn't register, and I don't really know how long I stood there in the doorway before he saw me.

"Mark, baby, it's not what it looks like," he started. Actually came toward me. And that snapped me out of whatever the fuck daze or trance I was in.

"What it looks like is you're moving. Or leaving," I said and backed away. I needed space away from whatever the *hell* this was. Wine sounded better and fucking better, and I turned my back to go get some.

He followed me out into the kitchen and watched me pour a glass and take a few gulps. I stared at the counter. He wasn't saying anything yet, but I was filled with anger and gloom. When I drained the glass for the third time, he reached out and took the bottle away from me. "Come on and sit down and we can discuss this," he said.

"This? This? What the fuck is *this*?" I stood there rigid, my voice almost a shout. "'Cause whatever *this* is, I'm pretty fuckin' sure I ain't gonna like it." Fuck, I hated it when I got mad. My accent went straight for the hills. That just made me madder, but it also made me get my shit together and do it quickly.

"Are you leaving?" I asked, point-blank. I stood still, watching him, waiting for the bomb in the room to explode and tear me apart. I should have known, I thought. Everything was going too well. I'd relaxed and stopped paying attention.

My mind jumped around everywhere while I stood there and waited and waited and waited.

Christmas was a miracle, I thought. Antonio's world hadn't fallen apart when he found out his son and ex-wife knew we were involved. In fact, he and Jason were closer than ever. Jeanine and Antonio had really talked, and she and Gary invited us to have dinner with them a couple of times to talk about whether to let Jason go out for football. It was freaky at first, I'll admit, and if I'd shoved coal up his ass beforehand, Antonio would have shit diamonds before the end of the first beer.

Jason stayed over more frequently and even spent a couple of weekends at my dad's house, getting into shit with his new BFF Robbie. Antonio and I talked about that relationship more than once, and while Jason had a girlfriend and was batting for the home team, I wasn't so sure he wasn't curious about the visiting one too. He was fifteen going on sixteen but not stupid. I remembered what made my dick hard at that age and cringed. I had Dad on the alert and Antonio covered his ears and la-la-la'd. Cute.

We'd gone to Charleston for his birthday. Spent a long weekend walking along the Battery and touring the historic district. I'd booked a room at a gay-friendly bed and breakfast, and we'd lain in bed for hours touching and exploring and making love. I didn't bottom often, but I showed Antonio how good it could be for me and for him to switch. He was such a patient and careful lover, and the lovemaking was tender and slow and so very loving. At the risk of sounding like a thirteen-year-old girl, I fell in love with him more that weekend than I thought possible.

His work was still sporadic, between massage clients and the start-up computer business he was working in fits and spurts. It was gaining traction, but his plans outpaced his ability to make them into reality sometimes. I spent more time at his place than at my own. My home became our haven when he needed to escape the ideas that got him in their grip and wouldn't let him go for hours at a time. I learned more about him all the time, and how his drive for perfection would frustrate him. Make him trash a project he spent hours, sometimes days on, starting again and again from scratch. I'd force him into the car and take him home and fuck his brains out to make him sleep.

For my birthday, he'd surprised me yet again. When I came home from the office, he met me in the parking lot and told me to get in his truck. "I just want to go take a shower and relax," I whined, not very manly, but he muscled me in and off we went. About forty-five minutes later we were in a small state park north of the city and in front of a small cabin.

"What're we doing here?" I asked, and was told to follow him in and not ask any more questions. When he opened the door, the whole inside of the cabin was lit by candles and a hot tub was softly bubbling. There was a corked bottle of champagne on ice and two flutes sitting by the tub. He even had my favorite Andrea Bocelli disc playing.

He undressed me without talking, then stripped himself. He took my hand and guided me into the tub, then sat on the edge behind me and uncorked the champagne. "I propose a toast. To my Mark, who showed me love comes from fucking unexpected places, and who makes me want to be a better man every day." After we drank, he cradled me between his legs and massaged my shoulders and neck while we soaked.

When he took me to bed, he laid me down and rode my cock until I couldn't take it anymore and I took control. I flipped him on his stomach and shoved a pillow under his groin to raise the angle and slid back into him. I drove harder and harder until he was begging me to come. When I lost it and shoved in the last few times, I felt him spasm around my cock and that took me over the edge.

Afterward, while I lay there with my head on his chest, he showed me my present. I'd been too preoccupied to notice it before, and it was a subtle but powerful thing. He had my name tattooed over his heart. That promise I felt to my core.

All of this and more flashed through my head and I started cursing. I let myself trust him. I built a family with him. I believed him when he said it was forever and he wouldn't leave me. I let my guard down and goddamn it, every fucking time I did that I got left behind.

"Just tell me," I said, suddenly just exhausted when it all hit me. I put my hands out on the island to support myself and stopped him with a glance when he moved to come closer. If he touched me, I'd break, and I needed to get used to it again. The not being touched. The alone.

He looked at me and started to talk. About the computers and the vision he had. "You know I'm really frustrated here in this shit apartment trying to do it and I just don't have the room and the materials." He started to pace around. I held on to the counter so I didn't just drift away.

"I'm really tired of doing massage and dealing with all the freaks. I want to do something with my brain and my talent, can't you see? I want to be something more than just this asshole loser who barely gets by." He stopped and looked at me. I waited for whatever he was saying to end. He started moving again like a caged tiger, around and around.

Seemed his mom called a couple of days before with an offer. Her brother was closing the family auto shop and the building was going to be vacant. Family owned, and all that space empty. "And all the good suppliers for metal tubing I need are right there, man. It's Silicone Valley." He stopped again, and I saw what I could only describe as yearning.

His mom, it appeared, offered him a rent-free arrangement. All he had to do was help drive her around to her doctor's appointments. "She lost her license again. DUI, three years this time." And there was room for Jason to stay on the holidays. She would fly him out.

Couldn't he see? Wasn't there blood or something all over this room? Because every brick he used to build this wall, this dream of his, was breaking my bones, crushing me and leaving me bloody and broken. But he just kept going.

He'd thought about it the past two nights. Funny, I thought he was asleep with me. *How stupid was I?* "I realized it would be best if I did this for a year, then could come back and have a better process down for construction and better components. I can work with the guys who do this shit all the time and build the company up and a customer base and we'll be set." And that's what snapped me out of my misery.

"We? There's no *we* here," I said. That pulled him up short. He looked shocked and stood there just staring, jaw working. "*We* means a couple who talk about important, life-changing decisions together. *We* means I get a voice and a vote in what happens and what affects me. *We* means I don't fucking hear about you fucking moving to fucking California when I fucking get home from work," I yelled. "*We means you don't leave me alone!*"

He had tears in his eyes. "Mark, I'm doing this for us. So I can be the kind of guy who's an equal partner, and Jason and you can be proud of me. I want to deserve you. I'm so tired of feeling like I am two clients away from having to ask you for more money to pay Jason's child support again. Baby, I want it so the only man I ever touch again is you. Please." He begged.

I was almost persuaded. Almost. "But you didn't want it bad enough to let me in on it, Antonio. My life is you and Jason now. You're leaving me," and my voice broke. I felt so empty, the life drained out of me.

He rushed across the room, grabbed me and hugged me tight. "No, no, no, no. I'm not leaving you. I'm just going to make things better. I'll be back before you know it. I promise," he said over and over.

"I can't do this," I whispered.

He let go of me and leaned back. He looked puzzled. "What? What can't you do, baby?"

I glanced up at him. "Am I going to be welcome out there? When Jason flies out, will we have family time? Will the three of us be together?" I asked, but I already knew the answer, and saw his face crumble. I knew he hadn't told his mother and sister about me yet. About him. Before this, they were a coast away. They didn't matter. But now they did.

"Maybe we can get a hotel," and he stopped when he saw the look in my eyes. He knew. The one thing I wouldn't be for anybody was a dirty little secret, and he just asked me to close the closet door behind me.

He tried again, "It's just for a year. Please, Mark, don't make me do this. Please," he begged.

"Do what?" I asked him. He cried, and it almost broke me too.

"Don't make me give this up. Don't make this a choice. It'll be okay, I'll make it work. Mark?" he asked.

I just raised my weary head and looked around at all the packing and chaos around me. I picked up my keys. "You already made it a choice and it wasn't me. You didn't choose me." I walked over to him and kissed his forehead as he cried then went to the door and let myself out.

"Mark, please. Don't you see, I am choosing us," I heard him sobbing when I closed the door.

I CALLED in sick for the rest of the week. Grabbed a couple of changes of clothes and my toiletry bag from the house and checked into a motel so nobody could find me. I was so drained, and I couldn't deal with anyone or anything. I turned my cell phone off and slept almost nonstop for the next twenty-four hours.

When I turned it back on the third day I had forty-nine new messages. I played them back, and deleted every one of his the minute I heard his voice. There were two from Patty, the first tender and worried, the second furious. One from Dad with a simple, "Call me when you can, son. I need to know you're okay."

The one from Jason was the one that made me sit up and take notice. "Mark, I'm so mad at Dad right now," he said and I could hear the tears in his voice. "Please call me. Please don't you leave me too."

Fuck.

My first call was to Dad to make sure he knew I was all right. I could hear Robbie in the background, talking a mile a minute and asking so many questions, Dad finally said, "Come to the house when you're ready to. Love you, son."

The second was to Jason's cell. "Where are you? Are you okay? Can you come get me?" he said all in one rushed breath.

"Slow down, buddy, I'm okay. I just needed to take a breather. Are you okay?"

For the next few minutes I was treated to a monologue that alternated between anger at his dad, fear and anxiety that I was okay and wouldn't want to be around him anymore, and a little excitement about going to California soon. He tried to hide it from me, saying he wouldn't go and nobody could make him, until I told him it was okay and he needed to see his dad. Reminded him his dad loved him.

"He loves you too, Mark," he said. I wasn't going to talk to Jason about that. That was between me and Antonio. It wasn't fair for him to be caught in the middle. "Come get me and let me stay with you, please, Mark, okay?" he begged. I hesitated, and asked what his mother said. "Mom," he shouted, and told her he wanted to come stay with me for the weekend. Jeanine's voice came on the line.

"You okay?" she asked.

Well, wasn't this fucking surreal? We were the ex-spouses club, because I ain't *nobody's* wife, current or ex. She laughed at that, told me to get my ass over there and get Jason before he took the bus. I wasn't going to let him take MARTA, so we arranged for me to come get him. "I'm sorry," she said before we hung up. "He can be a total dick and so damn selfish sometimes."

When I got there, Jason was packed and ready to go. He bowled me over in a hug and wouldn't let go. "I was afraid you wouldn't want to see me. You didn't call me back and I was so worried."

I pulled him back and made him look at me. "This has nothing to do with you, kiddo. This's between me and your dad, and whatever happens, you and me, we're good. Right?"

He nodded, and we gathered up his stuff and got in the car. God, it was hard to believe the little kid I used to know had grown into this tall and handsome young man. At almost sixteen, he looked so much like Antonio it hurt. The ratty little moustache was gone, and his features were sharp and masculine. He was starting to bulk up some. Playing football agreed with him.

He looked like he had something on his mind, and I figured he wanted to talk about me and Antonio. I wasn't ready to do that yet, especially with Jason. I needed to figure out where to go next myself. So it was a surprise when said, "Mark, I called Robbie and he's coming over too. I hope you aren't mad at me, but we wanted to talk to you. Um... is that okay?"

I'd had enough of wallowing in my own shit, worrying it over and over in my head the past two days. So it was almost a relief to have something to focus on besides Antonio. I cut my eyes at him. "Well, I don't know. Care to tell me what you two are up to? 'Cause you know, I may be old, but I ain't dumb."

He flipped his cell phone open and closed, his nervousness evident. I reached over and laid a hand on his arm and said, "Talk to me, Jason. You can trust me, you know that." I could hear him gulp.

"Robbie kissed me," he blurted out. "I liked it. We, um, well, we're kinda, I don't know what to call it, dating now? Maybe? We're still just friends, but...," he stammered out. Blushed, just like Antonio. Damn it. Thank God we were at a light, so I didn't drive off the road. I suspected a little flirting, but wasn't sure of anything.

"Buddy, we gotta talk. And yeah, he can come over. He's gonna talk too," I told him. And thought, *Holy Fuck, Antonio, you need to get your ass back here and help me with your son.*

When I got back home, I found Robbie waiting, looking really sheepish. I just looked at him a moment before motioning him to come in with us. "In, you two. Pizza or Chinese?" They couldn't decide so I called out for both. Fuck it.

While we waited, I sat them down on the couch. "Talk."

The two of them looked at each other and Robbie finally decided to be the one to speak. He took a deep breath and plunged in. "You know Jason and I've been good friends for a long time. And a few days ago, well... we were hanging out and just kind of kickin' it and I may have," and he looked everywhere but at me, "kissed him. A little."

"I liked it. I kissed him back. It wasn't his fault, he didn't make me or anything," Jason jumped to his defense.

"Guys, I get it. Okay? But Jason, you're, well, you're so young, and I know you're dating Amy. Just... be careful, okay. Promise me you won't do anything without talking to me or, oh fuck, Dad. Does he know about this?" I moaned. He went through this shit with me when I was their age. I remembered how mortified I was to have the condom talk with him. Fuck. Although, better him than me.

Robbie looked embarrassed. "Um, he maybe saw us kissing once the other day, and," he mumbled and shuddered, "talked to me about condoms and playing safe." He looked a little green.

That was it, and I lost it. Laughed until I had tears in my eyes and was holding my sides. The two of them looked at me like I just grew another head. When I calmed down, I said, through snorts, "I had that same talk when I was fifteen and came out. Did, did he use the cucumber?" Robbie's eyes were huge and he nodded.

"I can't eat salad now," he shuddered. "But Mark, I promise. I really like Jason, and, well," he looked over at Jason, who nodded, "I told Jason some things about my past. We want to take it slow. He's really special." He looked at Jason and smiled that secret little smile I knew so well. I'd been seeing it from my guys for years. Oh fuck, he was so done.

Jason looked back at him with the same look, and a cute little flush I recognized as Antonio's. I was going to have to watch these two really closely. They were already in love. I just hoped it if it blew up, or Jason decided girls were more his style, that he and Robbie would be able to stay friends. Because a friendship as special as they had shouldn't be fucked over…

Fuck. Fuck fuck fuckity *fuck*. God *damn* it. And I was supposed to be the adult here. I needed somebody to kick my ass. Something told me it would be Dad and Patty. God, I dreaded it. "Jason, where's your dad?"

He looked over at Robbie with a little *I told you so* look. "He's still at the apartment. Well, actually," and he looked up at the clock, "um, he's gonna be here in about an hour." He looked a little pleased with himself.

"Good," I purred. "Then you can tell your dad all about your little kissy-kissy with Robbie."

He gulped and went pale.

"Mark, can we… can we wait 'til we see what we want to do first? All we did was kiss a little. Dad will freak out and I don't want to add to all your problems. Please? I'll tell him, just not today. Please?"

I looked at the two of them and weighed it. I didn't like keeping secrets, but this one really wasn't mine to tell. If the boys decided to just be friends, there wouldn't be anything to tell anyway.

"For now. But guys, the minute it even feels like you two are going to do anything but sneak a kiss, it's done. Understand? I'm trusting you two." They nodded and looked relieved.

Then I got worried and excited and *fuck*. Antonio wasn't trying to do anything except better himself. I knew how he struggled and felt ashamed he wasn't making something more of his life. Especially when he looked at his son and felt… less than. Jason never looked at his dad with anything but unconditional love, but Antonio only saw the things he couldn't give him. Was it so terrible that he just wanted to be a hero to his son? And if I was honest with myself, to be my hero too. I loved him. The doorbell rang, startling me out of my thoughts, and the food started to arrive.

I spread a tablecloth on the floor in the den, put on *The Fast and the Furious*, and we had a picnic. I could watch Vin Diesel and the boys could watch the cars. Or Paul Walker, I thought. But probably the cars. We grabbed pillows and cushions off the couch and lay there on the floor, one of my boys on either side of me.

They jabbered, hooted, and laughed until I felt myself begin to relax again into my skin. When the doorbell rang Jason jumped up to answer the door. When he came back in, all I could see was Antonio. He sat down beside me on the floor and I noticed Jason and Robbie sneaking off to the guest room.

"Remember what I said, you two, and we *will* be talking later. Got it?" I heard "Yeah, yeah" from the hallway.

I turned to him, and didn't know what to say. When I opened my mouth to say "I'm sorry," he beat me to it. "Can you ever forgive me?" he asked. I reached over and pulled him to me and hugged him so fucking hard.

"If you'll forgive me for being such a dick," I said. He started to interrupt, but I stopped him. "No, let me say this. I'm not happy with the way things went down, but I promised I'd never shut my partner out again. If anybody needs forgiving, it's me."

He shook his head against me, but I kept going. "This's your dream. You aren't leaving *me*, you're chasing something for *us*. I want you to go. Just promise me you'll be back as soon as you can."

God. The look he gave me, so full of his heart and love. I reached over and turned the stereo on with the remote. Fuck, I forgot I'd left the "Lifehouse" mix with "Storm" in the CD deck. Our song. I pulled him up to his feet, into my arms and a slow dance. We had a lot more talking to do. About us, how we didn't talk sometimes. But we'd weather this storm. Everything would be all right.

CHAPTER TWENTY-ONE

June 2009

"ROBERT Allen Jennings." The principal's voice echoed across the field and we went bat-shit crazy. Robbie strolled across the stage with a huge smile on his face and turned to throw us a wave. That had Jason standing on his seat and hooting. Dad was almost as bad as he recorded the whole thing on his new PalmCam and grinned from ear to ear.

God, had it already been five years since this kid came into our lives? So much had changed since I sat with him at lunch that first day. And now he was graduating from high school. A year late, but after his time on the streets, I was so fucking proud he pushed through and did it. I didn't have kids, probably never would, but this must be what it felt like. We'd be doing this again for Jason the next day, and it would be special, but this, this was what pride felt like.

All of the family was out tonight to see him have his moment. He didn't know it, but there was a party waiting for him back at the house. A couple of old friends of his from Hope House were coming, and even some of his favorite staff. I had Jason call some of his best friends from school and they were going to be there. Patty had, of course, gone into Mamma Bear mode and organized shit even I didn't know about.

When it was all over and the caps were thrown and all the graduates were saying all the things graduates do about getting together over the summer and BFFs and Class of 2009 *rules*, we grabbed him and hugged the crap out of him. There may have even been some tears by the sisters. And me, dammit.

The boys were riding back with me, and somehow Robbie weaseled the keys out of my hands. Jason called shotgun, and I was stuck in the back. Those two always had their heads put together and tonight was no different. I kept seeing them glance back toward me and I got a funny feeling about this.

Finally Robbie cleared his throat. "Now, Mark, I don't want you to get mad or anything."

Shit. Subtle. "You better just tell me now. Which one of you thought whatever this is up and how much trouble are you in?" I asked. Another quick exchange of glances.

"See, the thing is, I know about the party tonight," Robbie said.

I glared at Jason. Traitor. "Okay, I'm not... mad. But at least pretend so Patty and Dad think you're surprised," I told him. "And you, I'll deal with you later," I said in my bad-ass adult voice to Jason. The little shit rolled his eyes at me. Robbie took a deep breath and started again, and I could tell how nervous he was. That made *me* nervous, so I leaned forward and tried to settle him down.

"It's not that bad—" I started and he blurted out, "Whatever happens don't leave tonight. Stay. For me. Make it my present if you want to but don't leave." And he and Jason looked scared. I sat back and tried to think what could have the two of... them... so... Oh, *fuck* no!

"Pull this car over right now. Robbie. Now," I grated out.

"Mark," he begged.

I was so fucking mad I could see red. He'd promised it would only be a year, but eighteen months later and still no end in sight. I wasn't even sure he was coming for his own son's graduation the next day. I was... hurt, ignored. And now I was furious. I'd managed twelve days and about three hours without talking to Antonio and I wasn't going to do it tonight, even if he had managed to get his ass home.

"Robbie, I'm serious. Let me out. I'll walk home." I started to take off my seatbelt.

"Mark," he said a little louder. I wasn't listening and wondered how badly I would get hurt if I jumped and did a tuck and roll thing like they did in the movies. My hand was actually on the door handle when he slammed on the brakes and shouted, "*Mark!*"

Jason was up and over the seat hanging onto me to keep me in the car while Robbie threw it in park and turned around. He grabbed Jason. "No, let him go if he wants to. If he's too afraid to face it like a man. Fuck him."

I was so stunned by Robbie, *Robbie*, saying that to me that I sat there, my mouth open. Jason let me go slowly and got back in the front.

"He's sorry. He misses you. So he fucked up? So what. I know he tried to call you every day this week and you won't even give him a crumb. You know what? You fuckin' aren't the man I thought you were. The man I knew was at the park looking for me at five in the morning when I ran away. *That* man forgave me for getting Brian killed," and he sucked in a sobbing breath. "*That* man had Zev put in prison when he tried to come back after me the last time."

I felt those words like physical blows. Black spots started to dance in the sides of my vision. A part of me was shouting, *Breathe, you fool.*

"Yeah, didn't know I knew about *that* little tidbit, did you? You think I don't talk to the boys I used to hang with? I know you called the cops the next day so I wouldn't have to deal with it, and they found all the drugs and the new kid in his house. You saved more than me, you big dumb fucker." And huge tears were running down his face. "So you fucking run now and all those other things you did for me that I can't ever pay you back for? Those things don't mean shit. You... your dad... Brian, you taught me how to be a man. So take a big shit on that for me, okay? Show me my hero is just a fucking coward. Okay?"

I didn't say anything. "*Okay?*" he shouted into the quiet of the car. Jason pulled him into his arms and hugged him tight against him, comforting him. The only sounds were Robbie's quiet hiccups and Jason's whispers of love and support.

"You—" and I had to clear my throat, "you've got that backwards, Robbie. You're my hero. Every fucking day, you're my hero." I reached up between the seats and pulled both their heads to me and kissed both their hair. After a long couple of minutes, I leaned back and put my seatbelt back on.

"Let's go home, boys. We have a party to get to. And I'll make you a deal. You act surprised and I will too."

WE STOPPED and got a couple of bottled waters and each went into the men's room at the convenience store to freshen up. We could always blame the red eyes on leftover emotion from the graduation, but I didn't want Robbie embarrassed.

As we pulled up to the house and stood by the car, I could see the party had started without us. I took a deep breath, pulled Robbie into a big hug and whispered for him to go enjoy himself. He looked up at me and I smiled. "I'll be okay. Jason, go send your dad out. We're gonna go take a drive and we'll be back later, okay." He nodded and jogged off to get Antonio.

"Mark, one thing I learned from you and Dad and Brian," Robbie said and bumped my shoulder. "Forgiveness. You showed me how. Man, if you love him, forgive him. Or at least tell him why you can't. But be honest with him." Then he walked away and left me standing there wondering when he'd turned into such an amazing young man.

I leaned against the car and put my head down on my arms to think over what he'd said. I'd been here before, I thought. My fucking pride had almost cost me Brian. And Antonio. When would I learn?

I felt him before I heard him though. All this time, and I could still feel him when he was around. "Antonio," I said without looking at him, my head still down.

"Mark," he breathed, inches away from my ear. I could feel him fight the urge to touch me.

Finally I looked up and turned to him. Pulled him into a hug and whispered, "It's still you. You're still that man. Am I that for you?"

His whole body sagged against mine, and I had to hold him up. I heard him singing something into my ear. As if he could still sing our song to me, this could be fixed. And maybe it could.

I WENT down the hall while Antonio walked to the kitchen to grab a beer. I heard a knock on the door and went to see who the hell was there. It was the boys. They pushed their way in and demanded to know if Antonio was still there and what was going on. "I'll tell you, but you better get back to your party, damn it. Dad and Patty—" I started to say to Robbie.

"Yeah, *they* sent us over here. Spill it," the obnoxious little fucker said.

"Yes."

"Huh?" Robbie said, looking blankly at me.

I said it again. "Yes, Antonio and I are gonna be fine." Then grinned. He slowly smiled, then grabbed Jason and kissed him. And not a friendly little peck on the lips smooch either. I felt like I suddenly needed a shower.

Jason flushed and pushed Robbie in the shoulder, and said, "Not in front of *him*. He's gonna tell Dad now." Then he paled and said, "You can't tell Dad. Please, Mark, let me tell him."

"It's about damn time. But one condition," I told him, about to lose it.

"Anything," he swore.

"I want to nuke some popcorn and have a beer and…," I said and they both jumped me.

When Antonio came back in, I held them to their word. I did exactly what I said I would do—made them wait 'til the popcorn was finished and opened a beer. Sat on the couch and motioned for them to go on. When they finished, he grabbed the beer and swallowed it down, then went outside on the deck without saying a word. The boys looked at me, crestfallen and near tears. I told them to just hang out and wait.

When I went out, he was standing, just looking up at the stars. It was warm and the sky was clear. I could see his expression in the light of the moon and gently told him, "It's going to be okay." He didn't say anything for several long minutes.

Then so low I could barely hear, he said, "You've been telling me all along and I didn't want to hear it. I didn't want it to be true." I almost said something, but decided to hear him out. He was so sad. "It's not that he's gay, Mark. I'm not a hypocrite. I just want him to be safe. You and I know how people can be, but we can take care of ourselves. Those two...."

I nodded and went over to lay a hand on his back. "Yeah, I know. Be happy they picked each other if Jason's going to be gay. We know he'll be treasured. And, Antonio, your son's in there right now looking like he lost his best friend. He thinks you hate him."

Before the words were completely out of my mouth he was in the house again, hugging his boy and telling him everything was fine, he was happy for him. He explained to the boys what he had just told me. I stayed outside and let him have the moment with them. I might love all three of them, but this was something a dad had to do.

We all sat down with Jeanine and Gary later that weekend and had the same conversation. They weren't surprised. Seems Jason sometimes forgot to shut his door completely when he had late night phone calls with Robbie, and it seemed they got a little... heated. If the two boys could've crawled under the carpet, pulled it over themselves and died, I think they would have. Antonio just made choking noises. I went into the kitchen and bit into a dishtowel to hold back the laughter.

We agreed that it would make us all more comfortable if they'd wait to take the next step until Jason was settled in at college. Surprisingly, they agreed. They'd already had this talk and thought they needed to be sure it was what they both wanted. Jason looked so much like his dad, ears burning as he admitted to being a virgin. Robbie looked a little embarrassed, and I guessed at its cause.

I laid a hand on his and said, "Robbie, it'll be your first time too." He looked at me, shaking his head, not looking at anyone, especially Jason. "Look at me, little brother." When he looked up into my eyes, I told him, "It'll be your first time with someone you love. If you two choose to honor each other, it'll be making love, not having sex."

His eyes teared up and he nodded, and gripped my hand so tight it hurt. "Thank you," he mouthed to me. "I love you."

CHAPTER TWENTY-TWO

March 2010

"YOU can open your eyes now," Antonio said. We'd been driving for what felt like hours and the blindfold idea was wearing a little thin. The boys hadn't been made to wear one, but all the bitching in the world didn't sway him. So I'd manned up and bravely sat there in silence the whole way. The three of them ignored me. Bastards.

When I slid the bandana off my eyes, I looked around and saw... holy shit but it was beautiful out here. The truck sat in a dirt driveway that ended in front of what looked like a two-story farmhouse. There were big century-old oaks, and azaleas lined the front, a mass of pink and white blooms. I could see that a small creek ran behind the house, and it was so quiet. Peaceful. There wasn't another house in sight.

"Man, it's nice out here. What're we doing here though? Ah, a picnic?" I asked as I saw Robbie and Jason grab a basket and cooler out of the bed of the truck. They laughed and bumped shoulders and moved to walk around the house toward the stream. I glanced over at Antonio and knew I must've looked totally confused.

He turned me to face the house and stood behind me, his head resting on my shoulder. "Tell me what you see, baby."

I took it all in, and said, "Reminds me of those beautiful old houses from the turn of the century that someone renovated into a bed-and-breakfast. It's pretty off the beaten track for that, though. But it's pretty as a picture out here. Kind of makes me think about the house Dad talks about his grandfather owning up in Demorest."

It started to dawn on me when Antonio laughed. "This is it, isn't it? This is the old Jennings farmstead? Damn, I wonder who owns it now. Think they're home? Maybe they'll let us go in and look around. Have you talked to them?" I asked all excited.

He laughed into my ear and kissed it. "You could say that, I guess. I have a key. Want to take a look while the boys set up out back?" I started to walk toward the house and admired all the care that'd gone into keeping everything looking original. And the yard was just fantastic. Antonio opened the front door and we went in.

The entire entryway and front room were heart of pine flooring and perfectly restored. The banister on the stairway going up looked to be stained mahogany, and the old-fashioned stair runner was embellished with tea roses. The front room to the right was lit up with the early afternoon sun, and I could just picture Dad as a little boy sitting in here with his grandfather, listening to stories and drinking lemonade.

We walked down the hallway and into the kitchen, and I was surprised to see the whole area had been gutted and updated with state-of-the-art stainless steel appliances. A great old plank dining room table offset all the shiny stuff though.

"Antonio, this's great. The owners really took care of the old place. Think they'd mind if we went upstairs?" I asked.

"Nah, let's go check it out." We went up, and I stroked the banister and felt how smooth and well-maintained it was. There were four bedrooms and two baths, all remodeled and decorated period. Except the master bedroom. It was redone in rich paneling and creams, with a fireplace on one wall, facing the king-size bed. I wandered over and admired the room, imagining the love here. And then I spotted the picture on the mantle.

It was me and Antonio. My arm around his shoulders, in San Francisco. I looked back at him, puzzled. "What's this doing here?" I asked.

He came over and gave me a quick kiss. "I bought it for you. It's yours," he said.

I laughed. "Well, duh, I remember when you bought it. That guy took the picture with your phone and you had it printed and framed for my birthday."

He pushed me a little, making me step backward. "No, you don't understand." Another little nudge. "I bought it." Pushed me and my knees hit the edge of the bed. "The whole thing." One last nudge and I went over backward onto the bed, and he crawled on top of me. "I bought the house and all the property." Kissed me. "On both sides."

The kisses made me fuzzy but I fought it. "Wait, wait. You *bought* it? When? How?" I managed to get out. He bent to kiss me again and I stopped him. "No, damn it, tell me what you mean."

He sighed and pulled back and straddled my hips. "Just that. I took part of the money from the buyout and bought this for you. For us. Now before you complain," he shushed me before I could get the words out, "it's a great investment. And I know we can't live here all the time. Your commute would suck."

He ground his ass on my crotch, and my cock decided to take notice. "Wait, stop that, *oh fuck*. I want to talk about this." He had other things on his mind than talking though, and as usual, I had to be the strong one. "No, baby, stop. The boys, if they come upstairs."

That froze him in his dirty little tracks. He fell off to the side and grumbled, "I should've sold him to the gypsies."

"Oh, I'll make it up to you," I said and groped him. "But, Antonio? This, this is… I just don't have words for it. It's a piece of my family's history. That you would remember and," I had to swallow down my emotion, "and want to make it a part of *our* family." I just shook my head.

"Baby, your family *is* my family now. I want the boys to have something that has some meaning to it. I didn't have that growing up, and I know Robbie didn't. You and your dad, you mean so much to all of us, and now that we have the money to do things," he shrugged, "I just wanted to make him happy. Make you happy."

"Thank you, Antonio. You *do* make me happy. Every fucking day, you make me so happy, I can't believe it," I said. I leaned over and kissed him and palmed his crotch again.

He pushed up into my hand, and I shoved a hand inside his jeans. "Think you can come in the next two minutes?" He groaned and nodded. This was my new favorite game. Giving him a time limit, and if he didn't get off within that time, he didn't get to. 'Til the next day. He'd gotten *very* good at this game.

I popped the button on his jeans and pulled his hard dick out. He lay beside me and wasn't allowed to move anything but his hips. I could go as fast or slow as I wanted but the grip had to stay the same firmness. He'd learned that if he timed it just right, he could get extra friction on the head when I went for an upstroke.

I glanced at my watch and grabbed his cock and said, "Go." He started to fuck into my hand, and I took a few slow, long strokes. Just to tease. His groan made me chuckle but he had some tricks of his own too. "Please, sir, I'm begging you. I'll be such a good boy for you." Ah, shit, that just wasn't playing fair. I jerked him hard and fast to reward him.

"Ah, fuck, sir, please let me come, please," he moaned and begged. My hand flew on his cock, and he started bucking like crazy into my hand. "Please... please... please," he chanted, and I let him off the hook, leaning over and catching his mouth in a kiss and stroking him hard and fast.

He gasped into my mouth. When his dick swelled and he shot, my hand filled with his load. I kept kissing him, drawing it out and bringing him down slow, until his breath was back to normal.

I got up and went down the hallway to wash my hands while he recovered. When I went back into the bedroom, he was still laying there watching me, eyes full of wonder and love. "What did I ever do to deserve this? Deserve you?" he asked. I sat back down beside him and rubbed his chest, thinking how long we'd waited to be together.

No one'd been more surprised than I was when I saw Antonio's truck, a U-Haul trailer attached to the bumper, in the parking lot when I came home from work right before Christmas. I went inside and found him asleep on the bed. When I sat on the edge, his sleepy eyes looked up and me and smiled a slow, lazy grin. "Merry Christmas, Charlie Brown," he purred out.

I bent over and gave him a long hot kiss. *"What are you doing here, baby? I thought you were working through Christmas and coming in for New Year's?"* He stretched like a cat and I appreciated the naked lines of his body. It had only been a month, but phone sex and video conferencing only did so much for a man.

"Apple bought me out," he said.

"You're fucking kidding me. They bought UnLinear? When did this happen?" I couldn't believe it.

"The deal closed and I got the wire transfer in for my stock package on Monday. They have some new product coming out in a year or so and caught wind of how I was using the caseless technology. They want it and the designs and they want it bad. So I told 'em to make me an offer. And fuck it if they didn't make me a damn good one. I took it and turned the keys over to them and packed my shit up and hit the road. I'm home, baby. For good," he laughed. I was kissing him so much he almost couldn't get the words out.

"That's the best news I've had in, God I don't even know," I said when I let him come up for breath.

"Well, you're kissing a very rich man. Guess," he chortled.

"Don't care." And I started to kiss on his neck.

"Umm, keep that up and I'll give you a blank check. You can be my kept man. Ow!" he yelped when I bit him.

"You're the one that's unemployed. I can support you, silly boy," I joked. *"You can lounge around in a jock and eat bonbons. Mmmm, I think I like that visual."* And I stroked my chin.

"We're rich," he said again, and leaned over and whispered a number into my ear.

"Shut up." I nudged him. *"Really, I'm fucking stoked for you, but no way they paid eight figures."*

He reached for the phone on the nightstand and handed it to me. *"Call the bank and check the balance in our joint account."* I decided to humor him, and dialed the automated teller. And dropped the phone when the balance was read off.

"We can do anything we want from now on. Buy anything. Help our families. Put the boys through school anywhere in the world. You can start your own nonprofit," he said.

"No, baby, this's your money. You earned it and—" I started before he put his hand over my mouth.

"Do you remember all those years ago when," and his voice cracked a little, "when I couldn't pay Jason's child support and you offered to loan me the money?" I nodded. He took in a deep breath." I think I fell in love with you that day. Nobody else in my life would've taken a chance on me like you did. I told myself, if I ever made it big, you'd be the reason. You were the first one who ever really thought I was worth believing in. Fuck, Mark, that gave me the balls to even try to get UnLinear started. You were my partner even then."

He looked at me and reached up to hold my face between his big, strong hands. "It's because of you. It's half yours. You were half owner all the time. Well, I always considered you to be."

I didn't let it make me any different. None of us did. I kept working with Hope House, and thought about what kind of charitable foundation I wanted to establish with part of the money. I remembered back to my best friend from high school who killed himself. My first boyfriend who died from complications from HIV/AIDS. Bullying of gay kids in schools was destroying a lot of young lives. All worthy causes. And we could fund them.

But there were two that we settled on. I picked one and Antonio picked one. Mine was liver disease, which stole my mom from me years too soon. Antonio picked brain tumor- and seizure- related studies. In honor of Brian.

Did I mention I loved this man?

And now he bought this beautiful place for us to bring back into the family. He was such a gift to me. I took him by the hand and led him to the backyard. I wanted to know how long those two brats had known about this, and how in the hell they managed to keep it a secret from me. But mostly I wanted to be with my family and share a picnic.

EPILOGUE

December 2011

THE church was full to the rafters, and it was truly beautiful this Christmas Eve. There were garlands and wreaths everywhere, and the entire sanctuary was lit with long, white tapers. The soft glow from the candlelight and the twinkling of fairy lights on the Christmas trees gave the space a gentle, home-like feel.

When I looked out, I saw all of our friends and family here to share the special evening.

I glanced at my watch and nodded to my friend Janet to start. She stood and moved to stand with the guitar player. All sound stopped and everyone rose.

I reached over to straighten Robbie's tie. "This is it, buddy. I've got the keys to the Porsche if you wanna run for it now," I teased.

"Shut up. I've been waiting five years for this day. You got the ring?" He worried and picked at imaginary lint on the sleeve of his tux. John Denver's song for his wife Annie was the perfect accompaniment to what we were here for.

"Of course I have the ring. Now turn around, here he comes. I'm so proud of you two." I squeezed his shoulder and turned him to face his husband-to-be.

"Robbie, he's so handsome," I whispered. Just like his dad.

He turned around and looked at Jason and Antonio coming down the aisle, and his eyes lit up with love and tears. "Yeah," he breathed as his breath caught.

"Fuck yeah," I agreed. Because I saw my man too.

Jason hugged his dad and took Robbie's hand and they moved to the left. Both of my boys were stunning in ivory tuxedoes. They only had eyes for each other though, and when my groom faced me in his black tux, the rest of the room disappeared for me too. I reached out for his hand, taking it and squeezing as we turned to face the minister and felt the solidness and warmth as he squeezed mine back.

Our families were here to celebrate with us. My dad, Antonio's mom. Jeanine and Gary. Patty. Robbie's sister, Angela. Even his aunt came. Everyone we loved.

We'd left three empty seats in the front pew. It was draped in Christmas lights, just like we did that chair at the dinner table on Christmas Day. A single white rose lay in each place for the loved ones missing in body, but there in all of our hearts.

Antonio's dad.

My mom.

And Brian.

T. A. WEBB is the writing name for the Mean Old Bear That Could. By day, he's the director of finance for a non-profit agency. He's worked with people living with HIV/AIDS and with children in the foster care system for over twenty years, and takes the smaller pay for the chance to make a difference for those who can't help themselves. After hours, he's the proud single papa of four rescue dogs, was born and raised in Atlanta, where he still lives, and is a pretty darned good country cook.

His sister taught him to read when he was four, and he tore his way through the local library over the next few years. Always wanting more, he snuck a copy of The Exorcist under his parents' house to read when he was eleven and scared the bejesus out of himself. Thus began a love affair with books that skirt the edge, and when he discovered gay literature, he was hooked for life.

T. A. can be found at Facebook under AuthorTAWebb, tweeted at #TomBearAtl, or if you really want to, you can email him at AuthorTAWebb@aol.com.